SEEDS
OF WAR

A JAMES FLYNN THRILLER
Book 4

R.J. PATTERSON

IMMINENT THREAT
© Copyright 2016 R.J. Patterson

This book is a work of fiction. Any references to historical events, real people, or real locales are used fictitiously. Other names, characters, places, and incidents are products of the author's imagination, and any resemblance to actual events or locales or persons, living or dead, is entirely coincidental.

First Print Edition 2016
Second Print Edition 2017

Cover Design by Dan Pitts

Published in the United States of America
Green E-Books
Boise, Idaho 83714

To my wife, Janel,
my greatest supporter and biggest fan

For you see, the world is governed by very different personages from what is imagined by those who are not behind the scenes.

— *Benjamin Disraeli*

SEEDS
OF WAR

CHAPTER 0

WHEN LI QIANG ENTERED the molecular biology and genetics program at Cambridge University, he wanted to help find a solution for world hunger. Despite all the backlash against genetically modified food, he held firm to his belief that the world's booming population couldn't survive without crops that had been enhanced in some form or another. And after ten years of research, his conviction had only grown stronger.

Yet when Qiang stepped into his lab on that overcast autumn morning, he knew he was doing the exact opposite—he was about to set into motion a global food crisis.

He wanted to stop, and at several points throughout the morning and early afternoon, he considered it. With a simple report, he could claim that the main vat for mixing Taranto's patented seed-coating formula had become contaminated. It would delay production by a few days, but nothing that would significantly disrupt the company's timeline for disseminating the product worldwide. While not a common occurrence, vat contamination wasn't unheard of. Staff workers would clean the equipment, remix the chemicals, and make another batch. But every time Qiang mustered up the courage to alert plant officials to the snafu, he thought of his parents huddled in a Siberian prison and decided against it.

It wasn't even six months ago when a Russian man broke into Qiang's apartment and jammed a gun into his back. The demand was simple: Contaminate Taranto's formula to render next season's corn crop unviable. And with more than ninety-five percent of the world's corn seed using Taranto's product, Qiang concluded such an act would cripple the global corn crop. However, it wasn't just about the food.

Corn's usefulness extended far beyond cobs for eating, popcorn for snacking, and the key ingredient for making high fructose corn syrup used to sweeten a plethora of foods. Medicines, makeup, adhesives, perfume, diapers, shampoo, toothpaste, and plastic bottles were just a handful of the everyday products people relied upon that were comprised of corn parts or made from corn. A shortage would have far-reaching damage on scores of industries.

Within seconds of hearing the man's persuasive petition, Qiang processed the extent of such an act before following up with a question he feared the answer to.

"Or what?" Qiang asked.

"Or else your parents will live out their days here," the man said, holding up a picture of Qiang's parents in a Siberian work camp.

"I'll see what I can do," Qiang said.

The man narrowed his eyes. "No, you'll do it—or else your parents will no longer be necessary. And trust me, you don't want me to use other incentives."

Qiang swallowed hard and nodded.

That confrontation was what led him to this moment, one where he steadily climbed the ladder attached to the stainless steel tank where the seed-coating formula was being mixed. With a half dozen vials tucked into his lab coat, Qiang neither looked the part of the saboteur nor would ever be suspected. Once he reached the top, one by one he poured the amber liquid into the vat, cursing himself for doing it. He half hoped someone would catch him in the act so he could come clean about how he'd been co-opted into such a nefarious plan. But such a hope was suppressed by his desire to save his parents, not to mention his own life.

As Qiang drove home following a successful mission, he realized the depth of devastation his own act would likely cause. Milling over the potential domino effect his act would result in helped him make sense of some other strange occurrences in the world markets, such as why the Russians had been planting wheat at such a high rate for the past five years. It was evident to him that it wasn't a hackneyed scheme hatched over a couple of bottles of vodka one night—it had been meticulously planned for years. The precision with which the operation was being carried out terrified Qiang. The only thing that terrified him more was that his parents' fate rested on his ability to comply with the demands placed upon him.

Driving along a two-lane road that wound its way through the foothills just west of the Alps, Qiang pulled over when he reached his favorite bluff. It was where he always went when he needed to think about a looming decision or find inspiration when his research had grown stale. He got out of his car and took a deep breath, inhaling the fresh mountain air. Then he dialed a number.

"It's finished," Qiang said. "It's time for you to uphold your end of the deal and release my parents."

The man on the other line laughed.

"You didn't really think it'd be that easy, did you?" the man said with a thick Russian accent. "Besides, what's to stop you from confessing to your plant supervisor about what you've done the moment I release your parents."

"Why would I do that? It'd mean the end of my career."

"Your career is likely over either way. I know you only did this out of your concern for your parents. And I don't doubt that you've been thinking about how you might correct this wrong."

Qiang seethed but remained quiet.

"I can assure you that they will be released and—"

Qiang listened in horror as two gunshots in the background interrupted the Russian man.

"I'm sorry," the man said after the gunfire. "There's been a mistake. They won't be released after all."

"But you said—" Qiang protested.

"I know what I said but sometimes thing change. This was one of those instances."

"I will make you pay for what you've done."

The man laughed. "I doubt that, but you go ahead and do what you feel like you need to do."

Qiang hung up and kicked at the dirt, sending a few rocks plummeting over the edge and down to the earth more than 200 meters below. He let out a string of expletives in both Mandarin and French. Then he dialed the plant supervisor.

"You need to stop the seed-coating treatment," Qiang said.

"Qiang? Is that you?" asked Marc Brodeur, whose presence at the Taranto facility pre-dated Qiang by five years.

"Yes, and this is not a joke. Please shut it down and dispose of the chemicals. It's been contaminated."

Brodeur surprised Qiang with a soft chuckle. "You mean the vat that you contaminated?"

"Wait. How do you—" Qiang shot back. "I thought—"

"You thought what? That no one saw you? I saw it all take place on the company's security cameras, but I deleted the footage."

"So you're—" Qiang said as he started to put it together.

"That's right. I'm working with the Russians, too," Brodeur said. "And once you're removed from the picture, we'll be able to blame the crop failure on you, disgracing your name."

"You'll never get away with this. I'll tell everyone."

"Who's going to believe a dead man?"

"Wha—"

Qiang heard footsteps and turned around in time to see a man rushing toward him. Before Qiang could get into a defensive position, the attacker slid a needle into Qiang's neck. Qiang collapsed to the ground before convulsing several times.

"I swear, I'm going to—" Qiang said as he clutched his chest.

It was the last words he uttered.

The assassin picked up Qiang and seated him in his car, slumped over the steering wheel. A heart attack for a hardworking man while taking in some of the area's breathtaking scenery. It would appear straightforward. No French detective would dare open a murder investigation as the autopsy would prove that it was just what it looked like—a heart attack.

CHAPTER 1

JAMES FLYNN STEPPED OFF THE PLANE in Longyearbyen and zipped up his jacket as he stared at the snow-covered mountains looming over the airport. The unforgiving wind gusted across the tarmac and carried loose snow with it. A handful of fellow passengers also making their first trip to the Arctic, and its northernmost permanent settlement of any significant size, gawked at the exotic environment and snapped selfies with their phones. With the sun hanging low on the horizon so early in the afternoon, the whole scene felt surreal to Flynn.

Before going inside to gather his luggage, Flynn surveyed his surroundings one final time and located the reason for his visit: The Svalbard Global Seed Vault.

When Theresa Thompson, his editor at The National magazine, called him into her office, he never knew what to expect or what corner of the country she'd be sending him to. Since the monthly periodical dealt exclusively with domestic issues, Flynn never imagined her uttering the words, "I'm sending you to the Arctic." But once she finished explaining her reasoning, it made sense to him.

Focusing on covering conspiracies, Flynn was no stranger to the one swirling around farmers and agricultural conglomerates such as the behemoth multinational company Fenestra. He couldn't casually peruse a conspiracy website without finding at least a dozen articles sounding the alarm against genetically modified food products, more commonly referred to as GMOs. And Fenestra was enemy number one. Then with biopiracy—the practice of stealing heirloom seeds for the purpose of genetically re-engineering them and then patenting them—among seed banks developing into a legitimate concern by those who donned tinfoil hats and those who didn't, Thompson saw fit to dispatch Flynn to pen a splashy feature on the subject. He would either quell fears or stoke them with his in-depth article. But either way, The National would sell out on newsstands everywhere.

"It's definitely not the Cherry Blossom Festival, is it?" said a man as he patted Flynn on the arm.

Flynn turned to catch the smiling face of the man who'd squeezed into the middle seat next to him on the flight. The man waved, and Flynn returned the gesture.

Forging ahead inside the airport to collect his luggage, Flynn was greeted by a mounted polar bear prowling across the baggage conveyor belt. The animal served as an iconic mascot for the Svalbard archipelago located a short two-and-a-half-hour flight north of Norway. But Flynn preferred to keep his encounters with one of the most feared land mammals limited to a long distance viewing, if at all.

Another man sporting a sweatshirt with the Illuminati eye on it approached Flynn timidly.

"You look familiar," the man said, pointing at Flynn.

"I get that a lot," Flynn said, trying to avoid a conversation. He looked back down at the baggage conveyor belt humming past them.

"Wait, you're that James Flynn guy on television, aren't you? The conspiracy hound?"

"Busted," Flynn said, shrugging his shoulders and cocking his head to one side.

"Oh, my God. You're one of my favorite authors," the man said as he pinched the sides of his sweatshirt and held out the iconic image printed on it. "Can I get your autograph?"

Flynn scribbled his name on the man's ticket jacket and took a quick selfie with him.

"I could get on a plane and go home right now because nothing out there is going to top meeting you," the man said.

The fuss he was making started to draw murmurs from everyone else standing around, though Flynn was certain nobody else recognized him. They all just wondered if he was someone famous they should've recognized.

Nope—it's only the fruitcakes who manage to find me in every airport on the planet.

Once Flynn gathered all his bags, he found a man holding up a dry erase board with "James Flynn" scrawled across it.

"Finn Larsen?" Flynn asked.

"You must be the man I'm looking for," Larsen stated as he offered his hand.

The two men shook hands before Larsen grabbed one of Flynn's bags and ushered him outside toward a van waiting at the curb.

"Welcome to Svalbard," Larsen said once he situated himself behind the steering wheel.

Flynn buckled up. "Thank you. Is this going to be a long ride to the hotel?"

Larsen laughed. "At the most, it takes ten minutes to get anywhere, unless, of course, a herd of reindeer decide to graze in the street. Then you're at their mercy."

Flynn looked north toward the water at the dormant harbor.

"Is that harbor still operational?" he asked.

His old CIA habits never fully disappeared. Whenever he went into a new location, he needed to know as much about it as possible, particularly entry and exit points. It was even better if the information came from a local.

Larsen nodded. "Not as much as it used to be with six flights landing here daily, but we still get several shipments a week."

Flynn strengthened his grip on the seat as Larsen barreled down the road, either oblivious to the icy road conditions or unconcerned with them. Regardless of the reason, Flynn's palms began to sweat.

"So what are you here for?" Larsen asked, breaking the momentary silence.

"I'm working on a story about the seed vault for a magazine." Flynn looked south toward the mountains and pointed. "Is that it up there?"

"That it is."

"What's going on up there?" Flynn asked, straining to see any activity at the base of the stainless steel door.

"At the seed vault?" Larsen said, breaking into a laugh. "Absolutely nothing. Nothing ever goes on up there."

CHAPTER 2

SENATOR DAN POWELL SETTLED into his seat at the conference table and adjusted the stack of papers in front of him emblazoned with the Department of Defense seal. As head of the U.S. Senate Committee on Agriculture, Nutrition and Forestry, Powell was used to enduring meetings that ultimately only seemed to justify the existence of the group itself. But this felt different. The California senator, who was gearing up for a nasty election to win a third term, perused a few of the documents. He leaned back in his chair, fingers interlocked and placed behind his head. The committee chair appointment was his way to gain influence and pick up a few perks from clamoring lobbyists along the way. Nobody ever told him that he might become embroiled in a homeland security threat.

"Do you have any idea what this is about?" Powell asked freshman senator Carl McCarthy, who was seated to his right.

"No idea," McCarthy said. "I had a private round of golf scheduled with the president this afternoon, so this meeting better be damn important."

Powell nodded. He hated meetings that felt like they were called simply to justify the existence of a certain committee. However, when General Morris Knight walked into the room, Powell realized it wasn't a mere inconvenience to his day because something serious was going down.

Knight pulled the doors closed behind him and strode to the head of the table, refusing to take a seat. He leaned forward, resting on his knuckles as he spoke.

"I'm sure you're all wondering why you're here today," Knight began. "It seems as though we've stumbled into some quicksand. And while it may affect you more from a political standpoint, I can assure you that this is not a subject where we need to try and carry political footballs with it."

Knight nodded at a man near the door. "Lights please."

A screen descended from the ceiling and came to a stop four feet off the ground. Powell rolled his eyes before closing them.

"Senator Powell, I suggest you sit up," Knight said with a sneer. "You're going to want to hear this, especially since some of your top campaign contributors are from Missouri."

Missouri? What does this meeting have to do with Missouri?

Powell shifted in his seat and leaned forward, hands clasped and propped on the conference table in front of him. It was an election year and comments such as Knight's weren't to be ignored. Instead, they were to be embraced. Powell was only at the end of his second term as a senator, but he understood Knight's comment could mean the difference in another six-year term or a return to the corporate world or a relegation to the academic community. Neither of the latter sounded particularly appealing to Powell.

"If you'll turn to page six in your packet, that's where the real meat begins," Knight said.

Powell hurriedly flipped through the documents until he arrived at the appointed spot and began reading. In the background, he could hear Knight droning on, but he was too mesmerized by the text on the screen that captivated his attention.

Executive Summary

As the spring planting season is now in full swing, there is an alarming trend taking place that must be acknowledged by Congress, which requires a contingency plan to be developed. As of April 26, not a single corn plant has emerged from the soil in the United States. Among the top 30 corn producing nations in the world, the U.S. harvests more than the next 29 countries combined. China is second on the list with 20 percent of the world's corn production. If this issue is indigenous to the U.S., only about a fourth of the world's major corn production will be available by the third quarter, leading to disastrous repercussions in our country and abroad.

Some of the potential results include the following:

1. Chaos in the world markets. Corn prices are projected to be as much as 100 times what they are today. The Chicago Merc might be forced to shut down.

2. Hunger and starvation. With farmers supplying their crops to the highest bidder, the product will inevitably fall into the hands of the corporations flush with cash and able to withstand a spike in pricing.

3. The death of thousands of U.S. cattle. Faced between feeding people and livestock, farmers will likely focus on people, who will shell out exorbitant prices to pay for food. The wealthy will also create a demand for premium beef, which could soar as high as $50 per pound for ground beef.

4. Bankruptcy for hundreds of restaurants and a spike in unemployment. With over 7 percent of Americans employed by the fast food industry, this could potentially devastate the U.S. economy.

The list continued on, but Powell couldn't read any more. Even to the uninitiated, it was clear that a catastrophic problem loomed. But Powell understood the far-reaching implications of such a paper, though one thing baffled him: Why was this a Department of Defense issue?

Powell raised his hand, drawing the attention of Knight.

"Senator Powell, do you have a question?" Knight asked.

Powell took a deep breath.

"This is completely disturbing on so many levels. Is there anything that can reverse this inevitable conclusion?"

Knight clasped his hands together and paced around the room.

"Good question, Senator. The problem lies with Fenestra, one of the groups you've been chummy with on the campaign trail—and in writing legislation."

"This isn't the time or place for politics, Mr. Knight," Powell said with a sneer. "Keep the commentary to yourself."

Knight smirked. "Very well. It'll be obvious to everyone by the time I finish talking or once they finish reading the executive summary."

"Out with it," Powell said.

"Fenestra, the leading agricultural company in the world, decided to ignore their pledge to the FDA to never breed their corn with the Terminator gene, which limits corn seeds to one growing season. Now, that might seem innocuous on some level since all corn seeds, whether organic or genetically modified, undergo a process of breeding in order to develop a batch of seeds consistent with certain characteristics and the seeds aren't retained for future planting. These replanted seeds would yield weak stands and be unpredictable when it came to their maturity. However, in the case of a near-global seed failure, it's important because even if a farmer saved his seeds, it wouldn't matter."

Knight stopped and glared at Powell.

"But, Senator, I'm sure you're very well aware of this practice."

Powell narrowed his eyes and shot a nasty look back at Knight.

"Anyway, the point is that we spoke with several Fenestra officials at their St. Louis headquarters, and they let us know that they broke that pledge due to financial constraints," Knight said as he continued to pace around the room. "Apparently, it was too costly to pay employees to spot check crops. So, they decided to take matters into their own hands. After all, if a farmer was infringing on patent laws, he's not likely to report anyone, is he?"

The room remained silent as Knight let his final statement sink in.

Powell shook his head as he returned his attention to the papers in front of him. As he continued reading the report, he noticed the perfect storm had commenced. Russia's overplanting of wheat resulted in a decrease in wheat production in the U.S. and an increase in corn planting. Once farmers planted corn and followed it with an herbicide, nothing else but corn or worthless sorghum could grow there. All sorghum was good for was chicken feed, hardly what U.S. farmers would consider replanting as it couldn't come close to replacing corn as it related to profit or usage.

"You're going to try and pin this all on Fenestra?" Powell asked. "Do you even know if it's their fault yet?"

Knight raised his index finger. "Another good question, Senator. We're still trying to determine that answer before we address the media on this matter, but their proprietary practices certainly haven't helped matters. All initial indications point toward a problem with Taranto's seed coating as the reason why the corn crop is failing. Unfortunately, more than ninety percent of agricultural companies that sell corn seed in the U.S. use Taranto's formula. That combined with Fenestra's practices sealed the fate of this year's corn crop."

Senator Gerald Doleman from Iowa banged his fist on the table.

"So, what you're saying is that there's no way the corn crop in the U.S. can recover?" Doleman asked.

Knight held up both hands. "Not entirely. There's still a possibility that it could recover sooner rather than later, though I think we all need to be prepared for a severe decrease in corn production."

"What does the Department of Defense believe can be done to stave off such an event this year?" Powell asked.

"This year is likely already lost, but we need to be thinking about the future right now," Knight said. "If we aren't able to secure seeds for this year, next year might even be worse. Shockingly, China isn't in a sharing mood, though thirty percent of their farmers plant seeds coated by Taranto."

"Let me get this straight," Powell said. "This problem isn't limited to this corn season, and the Department of Defense believes this might be an issue for future growing seasons?"

"That's correct, Senator," Knight said. "If we can't secure enough heirloom seeds, the kind that haven't been tinkered with in a lab somewhere, the future is grim. Right now, our projection models put us five years away from being able

to generate enough seeds to restore the current corn production levels in the U.S.—and that's only if we can secure
enough heirloom seeds immediately. If not, the projections
are far worse."

"Far worse?" Powell asked. "Who stands to benefit?"

"Right now, the only country who has a stockpile of
crops to feed the world."

Powell took a deep breath. "And who might that be?"

"None other than the Russians."

CHAPTER 3

Omsk, Russia

YURY GROMOV CROSSED HIS ARMS and stood on his veranda overlooking the Irtysh River. The water moved along at a swift pace, carrying anything in its path. He smiled as he watched a stubborn branch along the shore resist for a few moments before bending and succumbing to the current. Once attached to a healthy tree along the banks of the river, the stick was now at the mercy of the mid-spring flow.

"Do you always have to look so smug?" his wife, Irina, asked as she stepped out onto the porch with him.

He looked over his shoulder at her before returning his gaze to the water.

"Smug? Is that how you think of me?" he asked.

"I only think of you that way because you are."

Gromov smiled. "I guess there are worse things you could call me."

"Arrogant? Ruthless? Cold-hearted?" she said with a wry grin.

"That's how I paid for that necklace draped around your neck. Would you prefer that I were a much more principled man?"

Irina laughed and sauntered up next to him, placing her

hands on his chest.

"I like you just the way you are."

He wrapped his arms around her and pulled her tight against his body.

"Good because I'm not about to change any time soon."

She slapped him on the butt and scurried away.

He turned around in time to catch her giving him a wink accompanied by a come-hither look, making clear her desires for the rest of the evening. It was almost as if he were living in a dream.

When President Nestor Mirov approached him more than five years ago with a plot to help Russia reassert itself as a world power, Gromov didn't know what to think. He certainly never believed he could play such an integral role in helping his country climb to heights unseen in perhaps its entire history. Russia, or the U.S.S.R. from years ago, had once experienced a prolonged period as a world power. But those days had long since vanished. Russia was little more than a shell of its former self. Reduced in size and power, Russia was relegated to the role of a former beauty queen fighting to return to the spotlight—wrinkles and all. It needed more than plastic surgery to address its shortcomings; it needed divine intervention . . . or a deviant plot.

That help appeared in the form of President Mirov's plan, a scheme hatched out of brilliance, one that peered deep into the future and saw an opportunity in the making. If the pieces fell into place, Mirov could proclaim checkmate on the rest of the world and name his price. It'd make Russia not only a force to be reckoned with, but the force to be reckoned with on the world stage.

Gromov's participation was risky yet vital for Mirov's

scheme to succeed. As owner of Gromov Giant, one of the largest wheat planting and machine harvesting manufacturers in Russia, Gromov stood to gain from anything Mirov implemented. When Mirov shared a few of the plan's important pieces, Gromov agreed, blinded by the inevitable avalanche of money to be made off the deal. In essence, it was simple: Gromov agreed to ramp up production for his wheat planting machines, while Mirov promised to incentivize farmers to buy the equipment necessary to sow more wheat into the ground. Mirov even planned to subsidize the crop among Russian farmers.

To the outsider, it seemed like a gamble destined to fail. If the supply far exceeded the demand, what sane trader would be willing to pay full price for wheat? Such foolish initiatives would only serve to drive the price down and create a weak market. But Mirov explained to Gromov that his plan wasn't a short-term one but was of the long-term variety. Trust in Mirov was as important as anything in this venture, one Gromov felt confident would succeed. As soon as the Americans realized they needed wheat to feed both their citizens and their cattle, it was going to create a chaotic market, the likes of which the modern day world had never seen.

Gromov glanced at his phone and saw everything had already started to play out just like Mirov had predicted. The alert notified him to the fact that the American market had taken a significant dive—and it showed no signs of letting up.

For the past few years, Gromov felt a twinge of guilt for selling the state-of-the-art equipment to Russian farmers. If Mirov was wrong, it'd bankrupt every farmer he knew—and many hundreds more he didn't. They'd be stuck trying to sell the equipment on the open market, which would be depressed. And Gromov stood to lose millions. He closed his eyes and said a short prayer, not to any god in particular, but any one that would listen and grant him his wish: that Gromov Giant would make millions on the endeavor.

Leaning on the railing atop his veranda, Gromov waved politely to a handful of kayakers relaxing as the current along the Irtysh River carried them along. Up ahead was a patch of white water that wasn't easily tamed, serving as the demise for plenty of experienced boaters. He wondered if they were ready—or heading toward an early demise. He sighed and wondered if his immediate future held similar perils.

"Yury," Irina called from the doorway. "Are you going to come in or just stand there all night?"

Gromov hesitated, feeling as if the kayakers' fate was directly tied to his own.

"Yury, I'm not going to call you again," Irina snapped.

Gromov turned toward his wife and headed inside. Seconds after he shut the door, he could hear the screams coming from the river. He wanted to look over his shoulder and see what was happening, perhaps even help. But didn't even give the scene a glance.

His phone buzzed with a simple message that made him momentarily forget about Irina or the kayakers:

It's time to act.

Gromov dialed a number and waited through two rings before the man on the other line answered.

"Good to hear from you," the man said.

"Time to separate the wheat from the chaff," Gromov said. "Tonight is the night."

CHAPTER 4

Fenestra Seed Growing Facility
Raleigh, N.C.

NOAH BARTON GOT OUT OF HIS VAN and jammed his hands into his jacket pockets while surveying the fence in front of him. He'd spent hours assessing the security challenges facing his team at the Fenestra facility. And each time he did so, he wondered if he might be missing something.

Is this for real?

In a day and age where security measures were plentiful and relatively inexpensive, even a modest security system could deter potential thieves. For an organization that was flushed with cash, Barton was surprised that Fenestra didn't invest in something other than a ten-foot chain link fence, one roaming guard, and a pair of cameras aimed at the two entrances. Then again, seed-growing facilities weren't exactly high-value targets. That would all change by the morning.

Barton checked his watch and signaled with his flashlight to his two partners positioned on the far corner of the property. Based on Barton's reconnaissance, the guard at Fenestra's primary seed growing facility took a long bathroom break around 3:30 a.m. It'd be more than ample time for Barton and his team to complete their task.

"Let's do this," Barton said to Alicia Foglesong, his long-time girlfriend and partner at LES.

LES, also known as Liberators of Earth and Sea, never intended to turn to violence when it first formed ten years ago. The Earth Liberation Front and several other groups became synonymous with eco-terrorism. And Barton never saw violence as a productive means for changing people's minds. Yet over time, he grew tired of waiting for people to reverse course. He concluded most people were unable to think for themselves, blinded by competing slogans from wealthy interest groups that cared only about deepening their pockets. If people weren't capable of recognizing and caring about the reality that their world was dying a rapid death, he decided he'd help shake them awake.

When he first received a random phone call from a Russian businessman, Barton almost hung up right away. But he forced himself to listen and then do some research on the caller, a man named Yury Gromov. While Gromov's ex-ploits in business were well documented, so were his con-servational efforts—enough to get Barton's attention. Like Barton, Gromov explained that he'd grown tired of trying to convince people that there were corporations out there that cared only about profits, with the environment and the future to be damned. Gromov wanted to aggressively attack several of these companies, resorting to violent means if possible. And he believed LES was the group most suited to fly under the FBI's radar and make a statement against Fenestra and their practices of genetically modifying almost every organism planted in soil.

Initially, Barton remained reluctant, but Gromov prom-ised—and delivered—large sums of money. Barton figured the infusion of cash could help LES combat the special interest groups' campaign of lies on one front and deal a significant blow to its research efforts on another. So he agreed to work with Gromov.

The first target Gromov proposed were seed growing facilities scattered across the U.S. In these vast structures, companies could provide optimum environments for maximum crop yield. No pests and no weeds, perfect amounts of light and water. But inside grew the next generation of genetically modified crops, plants that would generate seeds to be planted as much as ten years in the future. Gromov explained that he didn't want to devastate every crop, just open the public's eyes about genetically modified corn. Wiping out these facilities would send the companies back to square one and educate the public on the dangers of genetically modified corn.

Barton couldn't agree more and assembled a team capable of carrying out such an orchestrated strike.

Alicia squeezed Barton's hand. "This is what we've all been waiting for."

They both scaled the fence and raced toward the building.

Ten minutes later, the entire team returned to the van and watched the flames lap skyward, consuming the facility.

CHAPTER 5

Koskov Mining Corporation
Barentsburg, Svalbard

EDUARD YOLKOV PLACED ANOTHER CIGA-
RETTE on his lips and stared out at roiling waters below
the ridge outside the Koskov Mining office. He didn't know
why he continued to smoke. Working underground in the
cramped ore mines led to a nasty cough, one that often resulted in thirty-second hacking episodes. He flicked his
lighter several times, but the wind squelched the flame. Using
his free hand to cover the lighter, he finally succeeded, the
tobacco assuming a familiar orange glow as it crackled to
life.

Yolkov inhaled the smoke before expunging it back into
the pristine Arctic air. The mere act of contaminating such
a majestic sanctuary might send some environmentalists into
a tizzy, but Yolkov wasn't enduring the bone-numbing cold
for the good of the earth. He'd lay waste to it all if it meant
he could get paid. Unfortunately, the only job he'd been able
to secure since getting kicked out of the Spetsnaz was with
Koskov Mining.

The Russian outpost on Svalbard had little to do with
gathering ore. Yolkov figured that out by the end of the first

day once he observed the paltry ore deposits returned to the surface for processing. Concluding there was no way the mine could be sustainable with such low yields, he began poking around, asking questions. He quickly learned that Koskov Mining was in business to prevent NATO from constructing anything on the Arctic archipelago that could target Russia or Russian interests—quite specifically, a missile launch site.

After his second week on the job, Yolkov had been assigned to take one of the company's snowmobiles thirty kilometers to Longyearbyen. The main reason was to purchase some supplies for the men, but the other reason was to make a sweep around the outside of the city and see if any new building projects looked underway. Yolkov had laughed at the notion given recent technological innovations.

"You find this funny?" Viktor, Yolkov's supervisor, had asked.

Yolkov had considered educating the frumpy man who likely wouldn't know what a launch site would look like if it was built on top of the Koskov Mining office. But he decided against it, preferring to do anything to get out of the mines for a day.

"No," Yolkov said. "I'll check the perimeter and bring back a full report."

Over time, Yolkov earned the assignment regularly, visiting Longyearbyen at least once per month. It felt good to utilize the skills he'd learned in the Spetsnaz, the Russian military's special forces. However, over time, they devolved into little more than days to get away from the mine. He readily recognized no country's military force had designs on constructing a launch site—or anything else, for that matter.

Even Yolkov could see Longyearbyen had long since ceased to be about ore production and had built a cottage industry catering to tourists who sought a different type of exotic adventure. But working for the mine was a job, one Yolkov needed to provide for his wife, Alexis, and six-year-old son, Boris, living in a small village outside of Perm. Yolkov's checks were split in half with one portion being sent to support his family while the remainder was held in an account until he completed a three-year assignment with the company.

With Yolkov's cigarette dwindling down, Viktor poked his head around the door.

"Eduard? Please come in."

Yolkov continued smoking until he took one final drag before snuffing it out on Viktor's desk.

"What is this about?" Yolkov asked as he settled into the rickety wooden chair and eyed Viktor seated behind his desk.

"I do not like being the bearer of bad news, but I have no other choice," Viktor began. "The mine has decided your position is unnecessary and will be eliminating it."

Yolkov let out an exasperated breath. "The mine has decided this? Don't try to act like you had nothing to do with it."

Viktor's eyes widened. "I swear, I had nothing to do with it. If it were up to me, I would have promoted you next month."

Yolkov shook his head. "Just as well. I hate working in this shit hole anyway. Just give me my paycheck and my voucher for a flight home and I'll be on my way."

Viktor took a deep breath and slowly exhaled.

"There is no paycheck."

"What do you mean there is no paycheck? I've worked faithfully for you and done everything you asked."

Viktor crossed his arms and looked out the window. "You have to remain employed with us for three years to earn the other half of your paycheck."

"It'll be three years next month. Can't you make an exception?" Yolkov pleaded. "I have a wife and son to take care of back home and—"

"No exceptions," Viktor said, still avoiding eye contact.

"You better not sleep tonight, you thieving bastard," Yolkov said.

Viktor pulled a revolver out of his desk drawer and pointed the gun at Yolkov.

"I suggest you leave now," Viktor said. "There is a vehicle waiting to take you to the Longyearbyen airport. Your bags have already been packed and are outside the door."

Yolkov slowly got up, but not before spitting in Viktor's face.

Viktor raked away the spittle from his forehead and motioned toward the door with his gun.

"I suggest you leave now before you make me do something else I might regret," Viktor said with a snarl.

Yolkov kicked his chair backward, knocking it over, before he turned around and strode toward the door.

"You better pray I never see you again," Yolkov said.

Yolkov didn't close the door as he stormed outside, taking long strides that sunk into the slushy snow. He pushed his way past a pair of men who'd been at the mining camp for several weeks and were filming a documentary on Svalbard. Yolkov overturned one of the men's coffee cups, setting off an exasperated rant from the man.

Head down and muttering to himself, Yolkov headed toward the main road where the cat tracks vehicles always picked up miners. But when he looked up, the only thing he saw was his duffle bag held by another man.

"Who are you?" Yolkov asked, snatching the bag from the stranger's hands.

"Oleg Dudnik—and I have a proposition for you."

Yolkov knelt down, unzipped the bag, and rifled through it to make sure all his belongings were there.

"I might be looking for a way to make some extra money, but I'm not into that sort of thing," Yolkov snapped.

Dudnik chuckled. "I'm sorry, but you have mistaken my intentions. I have a mission for you if you're interested."

Yolkov stopped digging through his bag and looked up at Dudnik.

"What kind of mission?"

"The kind that pays thirty million rubles."

Yolkov stood up. "What do you want me to do?"

CHAPTER 6

FLYNN LOOKED THROUGH THE PUB WINDOW at the people strolling home for the day along the snow-covered pathways with rifles slung over their shoulders. It reminded him of some post-apocalyptic movie where lawlessness ruled the day. He then glanced down at the menu and wondered how burgers and pizza had managed to proliferate even Arctic cuisine.

"Does everyone carry a weapon around here?" Flynn asked Finn Larsen, who'd agreed to dinner at The Arctic Barrel, one of Longyearbyen's more popular eateries.

Larsen laughed. "Why? Does it remind you of life in the United States?"

Flynn shot him a look and then broke into a sly grin.

"Americans aren't so open about carrying their weapons. They prefer to keep them concealed."

"Up here, if you don't have quick access to your rifle, it could mean the difference in you living and dying," Larsen said. "Polar bears don't wait for you to reload."

"So this is all to protect you from polar bears?"

Larsen nodded. "They tend to stay away from the city,

but if you venture beyond the city limits, it's against the law to not carry a high-powered rifle."

"Do you receive a fine?"

"If you don't get eaten first," Larsen deadpanned.

"So, who enforces these laws?"

"The Sysselmannen. Would you like to meet her?"

"A woman runs this town?"

Larsen chuckled. "Where have you been? Women run everything. What planet did you say you were from?"

Flynn shook his head and smiled. "I'd love to meet the Sysselmannen. Maybe she can provide me with some more background for my story."

"I'm sure she'd love to talk," Larsen said as he stood up. "I'll be right back."

A few moments later, Larsen returned with the Sysselmannen.

"James Flynn, I'd like to introduce you to our Sysselmannen, Kari Knudsen."

Knudsen leaned over the table and shook Flynn's hand.

"Nice to meet you," Flynn said. "Won't you sit with us for a few minutes and have a drink?"

Knudsen looked over her shoulder at her table, papers strewn across it.

"I have much work to attend to and came here to get out of the office for a bit," she said.

"Fifteen minutes of your time," Flynn said. "That's all I ask."

She shrugged. "Very well then. I think I can take a small break."

"And how about I buy you a beer as well?" Flynn asked as he slid farther into his seat, allowing Larsen to sit next to him and Knudsen on the bench across the table.

"Well, I'm no longer on duty." She closed her eyes and took a deep breath. "Depends on what kind it is."

"Oh, picky about your beer selection, I see," Flynn said.

"It's a must here in Svalbard," she said.

Larsen cracked a smile. "Or else you might find yourself walking home. Operating a snowmobile under the influence could get you a long time in the Sysselmannen's jail."

"Or deported," she said.

"That, too," Larsen said, pointing at her.

"So I take it you have strong beer here?" Flynn asked.

"Only if it's made here," Knudsen quipped.

"I had no idea there was a brewery in the Arctic," Flynn said.

Larsen leaned forward and looked at Flynn. "We only recently got one, but it got off to an interesting start."

"How so?"

"When the Spitsbergen Brewery held its first open house, it was a rush to meet the deadline. Unfortunately, the first batch that the brewmaster unveiled at a public gathering didn't have enough time to get the beer perfect. And it resulted in a heavy-alcohol beer. People couldn't figure out why they were stumbling around after a glass and a half."

Knudsen caught herself smiling before slipping her hand over her mouth.

"Were you there?" Flynn asked her.

"I intentionally avoided it. There are times when I prefer not to arrest my neighbors."

Flynn pulled out his pad and jotted down a few notes.

"So, is this a tight-knit community?" he asked. "Does everyone know everyone?"

"For the most part—or at least you have a general idea of who they are and why they're here," she said. "Tour guide, coal miner, hospitality worker, researcher—there aren't that many types of people who visit Svalbard."

Their conversation was halted when one of the patrons yelled at the bartender to turn up the volume on the television. The report was loud. Flynn found it unsettling.

"As markets opened in the U.S. this morning, the Chicago Merc plunged, nearly crashing as astonishing reports rolled in this morning about how the American corn crop is perilously close to being deemed a disaster. Both the NASDAQ and the S&P have dropped significantly as analysts are sounding the alarm and stating that this issue is no longer just a concern but teetering on a global epidemic. Over the past few weeks, investors and other interested parties along with the U.S. Department of Agriculture have been keeping an eye on the failing corn crop. Then last night, law enforcement officials in several states reported overnight vandalism at seed growing facilities, especially those owned or affiliated with Fenestra."

Flynn sighed. "And to think my editor sent me all the way up here—and it didn't have a single thing to do with all that chaos."

"It doesn't sound good," Knudsen said.

"Does the news ever sound good?" he shot back.

"You have a point," she said as she stood up. "Thank you for inviting me to sit with you for a few minutes, but I really have to get back to my paperwork. But if you want to ask me some more questions for your article, feel free to drop by my office during regular business hours and I'll try to make time for you."

Flynn thanked her for her time and assured her that he would be in touch. He then averted his attention back to the television where more security experts and agricultural experts were breaking down the impact of the report. After a couple of minutes, he grew bored with it all.

"The sky is always falling in America," Flynn said before taking another swig of his beer.

"How could you keep your people in line if it wasn't?" Larsen snipped.

"Very true. If there's not a catastrophe and people start to enjoy their lives, they just might forget that they need politicians to help them run their lives."

"Do you really think there's much truth to that report about the corn?"

"Why? Are you worried you might not get your allotment of corn on the island this year?"

Larsen laughed. "Close. I'm a connoisseur of popcorn, and I'd hate to see it vanish from the planet because of some bad seeds and some eco-terrorists."

"Corn is a part of all our lives, whether we realize it or not."

Larsen suddenly stood up and shook the hand of the man approaching their table.

"Mr. Runar Johansen," Larsen said. "It's a pleasure to meet you."

Johansen served as the general manager of The Svalbard Global Seed Vault, which was far from the baby-sitting project Flynn initially assumed it to be. As head of the vault, Johansen oversaw a facility that worked in conjunction with over one hundred countries and contained more than 4,000 different varieties of seeds.

"You must be Mr. Larsen," Johansen said before turning to Flynn. "And you're the reporter?"

"Yes, sir. I'm James Flynn."

"Excellent, gentlemen. Can we get started? I've got another meeting in about an hour."

"No problem, Mr. Johansen," Flynn said. "If necessary, we can finish up tomorrow."

"Sounds good to me."

Flynn scratched down a few notes before asking a few questions to get Johansen comfortable. While Flynn planned to ask about biopiracy at the facility, he wanted to build a rapport with Johansen first in order to get better answers to his questions.

"Are you stationed here on Svalbard or do you live in Norway?" Flynn asked.

"Oh, no. I live in Oslo. I only come up here when there are major deposits or to meet with dignitaries. Fortunately for you—"

Johansen stopped mid-sentence as a man stormed into the pub and started squawking to anyone who would listen.

Flynn leaned over to Larsen. "Who's that?"

"That is Vilhelm Madsen, the crazy man of Longyearbyen," Larsen said. "He's a bit of a mad scientist who works off and on at one of the research stations as an assistant."

"I can hardly understand what he's saying. Is it English?"

Larsen rolled his eyes. "It's a version of it."

Madsen raced over to the Sysselmannen's table and began talking excitedly.

"What did he just say?" Johansen said as he stood up and walked toward Madsen.

Flynn furrowed his brow.

"What's going on?"

"He said something about the vault," Larsen said while sliding out of his seat. "Just give me a moment and I'll find out."

Flynn didn't wait around, following Larsen over to the Sysselmannen's table, where Madsen talked hurriedly and expressively.

"Just slow down, Vilhelm," Knudsen said. "Take a few deep breaths and tell me again what you saw."

Madsen complied, drawing in a long breath before exhaling it.

"Now, very slowly, tell me what you saw."

Madsen swallowed hard before blurting out a response.

"I was out at the airport and looked up toward the mountains. Someone is breaking into the seed vault!"

CHAPTER 7

Washington, D.C.

SENATOR POWELL SLUMPED into his chair and exhaled. He had plans for the weekend, plans that included taking advantage of Fenestra's chalet in the Swiss Alps and disappearing from the public eye. It was the kind of trip he needed for his sanity, not to mention for his future political aspirations. His brief military background landed him on the U.S. Senate Committee on Armed Services and that was where the real power was. He'd already begun to liaison with Anders Pedersen, a Norwegian Lieutenant General who directed a NATO black ops program based out of Kirkenes. While Powell was in Switzerland, he planned to meet with Pedersen to discuss some of the Scandinavian region's growing concerns about aggressive Russian activity.

But Powell knew it was a trip—and a meeting—that would have to wait.

He logged onto his computer and checked the stock market. The arrow designating the direction of the stocks that day pointed downward and in a sharp descent. There was no soft landing to be had. Stocks were going to bottom out with a resounding thud. And there wasn't much anyone could do about it other than pray for the final bell over the weekend to ring early.

That wasn't going to happen either.

After a few minutes of scrambling around, he called the CIA and reached the deputy director, Nelson Gilbert.

"Do you realize what's happening as we speak?" Powell asked.

"I've been watching the news. Is it as bad as they're making it out to be?" Gilbert said.

"It's worse. Much worse."

"What do you mean?"

Powell sighed. "I received a call this morning, pulling me into an emergency conference call with the Chairman of the Joint Chiefs of Staff and several others regarding this debacle with the corn crop. And believe you me, it's about to send this nation into a panic, the likes we haven't seen since The Great Depression."

"That bad?"

"Perhaps or maybe even worse. It's too early to tell."

"Is there any way we can help?"

"I'm sure your boss will notify you quickly if there are any actionable steps you can take, but for now we're in lockdown mode when it comes to corn seed."

Gilbert was quiet for a moment. "So it's as serious as it sounds?"

"Maybe even more so. If we can't secure heirloom corn seeds, it may be several years before we get our corn crop back on track."

"So, these aren't just conspiracy nut alarmists?"

"When you consider that we produce more than a third of the corn grown annually in the world and how corn comprises so many products we consume daily, not to mention food, it's easy to see that we're headed for a agricultural armageddon."

Gilbert groaned. "And who produces the second most acres of corn?"

"Our wonderful neighbors, China."

"They're going to enjoy this, aren't they?"

Powell laughed. "They might be in the same predicament we are since they get plenty of their seeds from the same place."

"And Russia?"

"They're sitting on a stock pile of wheat, the only crop that can help assuage the damage caused by a corn shortage—even though it won't fully make up for the damage. Either way, we're screwed."

"So you want the CIA to help you secure all the heirloom corn seed?"

Powell sighed. "If it were only that easy. Over the past month, one of those eco-terrorism groups has been hitting seed vaults across the U.S. and stealing only corn seeds. That should've clued someone in at the USDA that there was some monkey business going on, but I didn't hear a peep of it in our security briefing. That seemed to only be relevant today."

"What are you calling me for then?"

"There is one more vault left that they haven't hit to our knowledge," Powell said.

"And that is?"

"The Svalbard Global Seed Vault."

"Only the most difficult vault to break into in the world."

"Or so they say. Look, it doesn't matter. We just need to

get someone up to the Arctic to secure that corn. According to the USDA chief, we've got two bags of corn stored up there. Under the proper conditions, we might be able to use that seed to get things turned around so this corn shortage only lasts a year. It'll hurt us in the short term, but we'll recover quickly—as long as we're able to secure that corn."

"We don't exactly have agents up there, Senator. That's not the kind of place we go to assess security threats."

"I understand, but can you make a few calls and find out for me? Or else we're going to need to dispatch someone up there immediately."

"I'm on it," Gilbert said.

Five minutes later, Powell's phone rang. It was Gilbert.

"You're in luck, Senator," Gilbert began. "Seems like we happen to have a guy up there already. Though, he's not really one of ours, but a former operative by the name of James Flynn."

"That'll work. Can you give me his number?"

"Yeah, I'm about to text it to you. Make sure you let Flynn know that you got his number for Todd Osborne at the CIA. Flynn didn't exactly leave on good terms, but he's been helpful in several off-book operations since then."

Powell drummed his fingers on his desk.

"So, he likes to go rogue?"

"Nothing like that," Gilbert said. "But he's definitely your guy in a pinch."

"I'd say this qualifies for a pinch."

"And for much more based on what I'm reading."

"Thanks for the contact. I'll brief you on my conversation with him so you can take it from there."

"You sure you don't want us to contact him first?"

"I want to speak with him first," Powell said. "He needs to understand just how important this is."

"Senator, it's just retrieving some seeds from a vault, seeds that we own. How difficult can it be?"

"If there's one thing I've learned after being in politics for nearly four decades, it's that things never go as planned."

***

FLYNN GLANCED AT HIS PHONE as he grabbed his coat and joined a trio of vehicles. Vilhelm Madsen led the pack, followed by Knudsen and Johansen in the Sysselmannen's SUV and Larsen and Flynn in Larsen's Forerunner.

"Do you need to get that?" Larsen asked after Flynn's phone rang for the fifth time.

"I don't recognize the number, but it must be important," Flynn said. "This is the second time they've called."

Larsen jerked the wheel hard to the left, tossing Flynn against the passenger side door.

"Sorry, mate," Larsen apologized. "We're in a bit of a hurry."

Flynn answered the phone.

"Is this James Flynn?" asked an unfamiliar voice on the other end.

"Yes. Who's this?"

"My name is Senator Dan Powell—and I have an urgent request for you."

"I'm afraid there must be some mistake, Senator. I no longer work for the U.S. government."

Larsen shot Flynn a look before Flynn waved him off as if it wasn't important.

"That doesn't matter to me, Mr. Flynn. This is a matter of national security."

"Go on."

"I doubt you've heard, but there is a looming crisis in the U.S. as we speak."

Flynn grunted as Larsen flew through another intersection and slammed Flynn against the door.

"Are you talking about the issue with the corn?"

"You already heard about it up there?"

Flynn chuckled. "People have televisions and internet here, Senator. They don't live in igloos and work on whaling boats. This is the 21st Century."

"Whatever. The point of my call is that Todd Osborne suggested your name."

"Good ole Todd, always ruining my work day."

"I apologize for the interruption, Mr. Flynn, but we need your help."

"Just spit it out already."

"We need you to secure about eighty pounds of heirloom corn seed that the U.S. has donated to the seed vault there."

"Senator, you are aware that I'm only allowed fifty pounds per checked bag," Flynn said, breaking into a smile.

"Mr. Flynn, this is a serious matter. If you don't secure those seeds, we could be looking at far-reaching financial repercussions in the U.S. and worldwide. Aside from there not being enough food to eat, animals are going to die, business will have to let people go—and people are going to die."

"Senator, I think I can help you sooner than you think."

"How's that?"

"We're on our way to the seed vault right now with the director of the vault along with the Sysselmannen."

"The syssel-who?"

"Never mind, Senator. It's not important. Just know that I'll be in the vault in a matter of minutes and should be able to secure the corn then."

"Please call me the moment you have your hands on it."

"Will do."

Flynn hung up and looked at Larsen.

"I hope I didn't just make a promise that I can't keep."

CHAPTER 8

The Global Seed Vault
Longyearbyen, Svalbard

YOLKOV HAD A SIMPLE MISSION: Get into the vault, grab all the U.S. corn seed, and get out. For thirty million rubles, Yolkov thought he would've had to assassinate a foreign diplomat or plant a bomb in enemy territory. But grab a few bags of corn seed? Yolkov couldn't believe he'd fallen into such good fortune.

This was the kind of mission his Spetsnaz training prepared him for. Opening doors that were supposedly secured happened to be his specialty. When President Putin called on the Spetsnaz to rescue the 850 hostages held by Chechen rebels in Moscow at the Dubrovka Theater in 2002, Yolkov was the munitions specialist who helped blow the doors off a section of the theater. His work gave the Spetsnaz access to the main auditorium to rescue the hostages.

While Dudnik warned Yolkov that the Svalbard Global Seed Vault contained one of the world's premier security systems in the world, he laughed the man off. He wouldn't be intimidated by such designations, which he knew were little more than trumped up marketing material verbiage. If this was indeed a doomsday vault as many people called it, what good would it possibly be if a true apocalypse took place and nobody couldn't get inside? Gaining access had to be easier than breaking into the Kremlin.

The only thing Yolkov didn't count on while standing atop the mountain was that someone would see him.

Yolkov knew the drill at the Longyearbyen airport. The 2:45 p.m. flight was the last of the day, until another flight arrived some time around midnight. Between 4:00 p.m. and 10:00 p.m., the airfield was virtually vacant. And this was important because aside from the sparse dock activity at the water's edge, the seed vault was only visible to people working in those two locations. Even with twenty-four-hour sunshine, Yolkov wasn't concerned that he'd be spotted. He figured he had a better chance of seeing a polar bear roaming around than he did a person during that window of time.

He drove his snowmobile up the snow-covered road that wound up the mountain. The road didn't stop at the vault, but it might as well have. Only mining vehicles and utility trucks ventured farther down the road. But like most days, it was desolate.

When Yolkov reached the vault, he drove up the embankment behind the entrance and parked his snowmobile behind a large snowdrift, hiding the vehicle from plain view. He grabbed his satchel full of tools, slinging it over his shoulder. Yolkov scanned the surrounding area once more with his binoculars to make sure no one was watching him. It was quiet, save the incessant wind that came howling down the mountain, carrying loose snow

Perfect.

Yolkov got to work, assessing the locks on the double doors that sat at the bottom of a steel box that towered ten meters into the air. At the top quarter of the box was a design containing large shards of blue and green glass. To the uninitiated, the structure jutting out of the mountain face appeared little more than a piece of modern art, belying what rested inside.

But Yolkov wasn't interested in anything but how to gain access to the facility. All that stood between him and the inside were two deadbolt locks. Not even a visible security camera.

In a matter of minutes, he'd picked both locks and was inside. He descended a short ramp that led him deeper into the mountain where he ran into another lock and a keypad. Debating which tool to utilize, he decided a more direct approach would be the most expedient, even if it would alert the authorities to an intruder. In less than a minute, he'd set a charge and run up the ramp to avoid any shrapnel once the door blew open.

Boom! A small puff of smoke hovered near the door for a few moments. Yolkov hustled back down the ramp as he figured he had no more than ten minutes before someone would be investigating the scene. Not that he was too worried, but he preferred a clean getaway to a messy one. However, for thirty million rubles, he wouldn't be too picky if forced to choose.

Yolkov spent a minute assessing the organizational layout of the vault, trying to identify as quickly as possible where the U.S. seeds were. Once he located them, he began searching for the corn seeds. He identified two large containers near the top shelf that required him to use a ladder to reach them. Hustling around the vault, he found a large ladder with wheels that he rolled into place. He climbed the steps, grabbed the two boxes, and brought them down.

After opening the containers, Yolkov decided to combine the contents of the two containers into one for easier handling on his snowmobile. When he finished, he knocked over a few other seed containers, making the theft seem a little more random.

He ripped open a container from North Korea and another from Moldova. The English, the Saudis, the Chinese—Yolkov didn't play favorites. Then he was out of the room, sprinting up the ramp toward his snowmobile.

As soon as he finished securing the container onto the back of his snowmobile, Yolkov looked down the mountain and saw the Sysselmannen's SUV turn onto the road leading to the vault and roar up it, while another vehicle followed close behind.

I should've known it wasn't going to be that easy.

CHAPTER 9

FLYNN LOOKED AT LARSEN, whose eyes bounced between the road and his passenger. The director and the Sysselmannen blew through a stop sign, sliding to the edge of the groomed icy road. Larsen followed suit.

"I know this is an emergency situation, but it seems like you guys are always driving like this—or is that just my imagination?" Flynn asked.

As he drove along, Larsen kept ping-ponging between Flynn and the road.

"What?" Flynn said. "You keep looking at me like you just invited some cold-blooded killer to sit next to you. Are you that scared of me?"

"Depends."

"On what?"

Larsen's knuckles whitened as he glanced over at Flynn.

"Are you really CIA?"

Flynn broke into a hearty laugh. "Seriously? That's what you're so worried about?"

Larsen's eyes widened. "I've seen the movies. Those guys are badass killers who—"

Flynn smiled and shook his head. "Just relax. I'm not here for you. Besides, you're an adventure guide. You can handle yourself, right?"

"Maybe against a polar bear attack."

"I promise you I'm less fierce than a polar bear. Plus I'm a little rusty. It's been a while since I worked for the CIA."

Larsen tried to keep pace with the Sysselmannen.

"So, do you have a weapon?" Flynn asked.

"I've got several in the back. Take your pick. All the ammunition is in the console."

Flynn pulled out a semi-automatic Falkor Petra and admired it for a moment.

"May I?" he asked.

"Be my guest," Larsen said. "I've got a whole arsenal in the back. And so does the Sysselmannen. If you want to see another gun—"

"No, this is perfect," Flynn said with a smile.

They turned the corner and roared up the hill toward the vault. The place appeared deserted.

"Does anyone come up here every day?" Flynn asked.

"It's a vault in the truest sense of the word," Larsen said. "The director comes up every few months with some dignitaries or when a major deposit is scheduled. But for the most part, it just sits on the side of the mountain."

"Good. We won't have to worry about any hostage situations developing then."

Larsen shrugged. "Except for the seeds, right?"

"I doubt it'll be much of a problem."

Larsen leaned forward over the steering wheel, peering up at the vault's entrance.

"It won't be much of a problem at all if he isn't even here."

Flynn joined him, looking up the mountain.

"What do you mean?"

"It doesn't look like there's anyone up there," Larsen said, gesturing toward the vault. "I know whoever was doing this isn't stupid enough to try to make a getaway on foot, but I don't see a truck or a snowmobile anywhere."

"Could he have parked inside?"

"Maybe, but I doubt it. Seems like a crazy thing to do."

Flynn scanned the area as they drew closer.

"The truth is, we're flying blind right now. Whoever this guy is has to have extensive knowledge of the terrain and a plan. We're just up here trying to contain the situation. He's got the advantage over us, for sure."

"I know all about this place—and so does the Sysselmannen."

Flynn shot Larsen a look. "But have you ever planned an op? You don't just snap your fingers and come up with a plan. Unless you get a heavy dose of good luck—or bad luck, depending on how you see things—you're almost always going to lose out if the other party has a solid plan and decent skills."

"It's probably some dumb Russian."

"I'd bet my life on the fact that it's a Russian—but I promise you, he's not dumb."

Larsen came to a halt, parking next to the Sysselmannen. Both Larsen and Flynn sprang open their doors and jumped out of the SUV. Flynn checked his weapon and looked at the Sysselmannen.

"How do you want to handle this?" Flynn asked.

She gave him the once over, stopping on his weapon.

"Is there something about you I need to know?" she asked.

Larsen didn't give Flynn a chance to answer. "He's former CIA."

"Former CIA?" she said. "I never would've guessed it."

Flynn furrowed his brow. "Really?"

"Get over yourself," she said. "I'll take the lead. Let's try to clear the vault. Director, you stay in the car. Larsen, you get behind our truck and take him out if he comes flying out before us."

"Shouldn't we secure the premises first?" Flynn asked.

Knudsen stopped and put her hands on her hips. She swiveled her head back and forth a few times, looking around the side of the mountain.

"Do you see anything other than ice and snow on this mountainside?" she asked.

Flynn shook his head. "No, but it's always good to—"

She waved him off. "Forget it. There's nowhere to hide around here. There's a good chance he's already gone."

"What about those tracks right there?" Flynn said, pointing toward a pair of footprints heading up the mountain.

"Those?" she said, pointing at them and laughing. "If he made it over the ridge already, we'll never catch him. He's probably halfway back to Barentsburg or wherever the hell he's going."

"This is your island," Flynn said, relenting and falling in line behind her.

They walked through the open doors and tried to steady themselves down the sloped entryway toward the inner door, which hung open as well.

"Let's fan out," she said. "I'll go left. You go right."

"Roger that," Flynn said.

As they entered the vault area, they split up. Flynn

walked down several aisles and saw nothing.

"Clear," he yelled.

"Clear," she answered back.

Knudsen walked down one aisle where she noticed some seeds on the ground.

"Come here and take a look at this."

Flynn jogged in the direction of her voice until he found her.

"Looks like he took all the corn seed. We won't be growing a single stock of corn for a long time unless we catch this guy."

"The director isn't going to like this," she said.

"Neither are the people in Washington."

They both made one last scan of the place but found nothing.

"Let's go give the director the bad news," she said.

"Better the director than the senator I have to call. He might start throwing things."

She smiled. "At least he can't throw them at you here in the Arctic."

They walked up the ramp and outside into the wind.

"Did you see anything while we were in there?" Knudsen asked Larsen.

He shook his head. "It was quiet out here."

Flynn froze. "Did you hear that?"

"Hear what?" Knudsen asked.

He heard the sound of an engine.

"That," he said, pointing up the mountain. "You don't hear it."

She shook her head and then stopped.

"Wait. I think I hear something."

The hum turned into a roar that sounded like it was coming right toward them.

Flynn looked up along with Knudsen and Larsen as a snowmobile hurtled over the top of the roof and hit the ground twenty meters away from them, tearing down the mountainside.

CHAPTER 10

Omsk, Russia

GROMOV POURED HIMSELF a glass of wine and awaited the good news. He expected to hear from his contact on Svalbard at any moment. In the meantime, he started to pace around the living room in front of the television, which was on an international news channel. The report—and the wine—calmed his nerves.

Officials on the New York Stock Exchange decided to close the market early Friday as stocks plunged on the news that more than ninety percent of the U.S. corn crop may fail this year. Investors in products that utilize corn remained nervous, with many pulling out within minutes of the news breaking. Meanwhile, food products that didn't require corn surged. In other news . . .

Gromov wanted to smile. He wanted to toast his good fortune and celebrate with his wife. Perhaps he'd buy her a private island off the coast of Italy. Or they'd vacation for a month in Dubai with VIPs and movie stars. By Russian standards, they'd always been wealthy. But he was about to be rich by the world's standards—filthy rich. Whatever he wanted, he'd get. The same went for Irina. He knew she'd always wanted a bigger diamond for her wedding band—

and a matching necklace. No longer would those be dreams; it'd be their everyday reality.

He stopped short his trip to fantasyland to focus on the issues that needed to be dealt with before anything else happened. Once the U.S. corn seed was in the possession of the Russian army on board the K-329 Severodinsk submarine, he might relax.

Despite his best efforts to suppress it, he couldn't resist the natural high that came with succeeding in a plot to restore his homeland to national prominence. The residual effects served as a simple payoff for his loyalty. He always believed Russia would regain its rightful place in the world. After the breakup of the USSR, they'd all suffered. Whether it was the public scorn from the rest of the world or the shame that the country was a "shell of its former self," Russians were all struggling to survive under the weight of failed government policies. It didn't matter—not anymore, anyway. Russia was primed to rise from the ashes and rule once again, this time with a harsher gavel.

Even with all the information he'd been privy to, Gromov went all in, even buying futures of Chinese corn. He was about to turn his fifty thousand dollar investment into a five million dollar payday. It'd be pocket change compared to how he was about to cash in with the rest of the market, but it'd be a slick story he could tell magazines and newspapers when they interviewed him regarding his rise to power and fortune.

Gromov wanted to run out onto his veranda and shower himself with cash, basking in the moment. But he couldn't. He had to wait. And he couldn't wait any longer.

"What's happening, Berezin?" Gromov asked once the

Russian commander answered his phone. Nikolai Berezin was one of the best submarine commanders in the Russian Army and his tolerance for incompetency was almost non-existent.

Berezin grunted. "I told you that I'd call you once everything was secured."

"So, it's still not secured? What's the problem?"

"There is no problem," Berezin snapped. "The operative let me know that he's secured the package, but I've yet to see it."

"You don't think he's going to try and bid it up, do you? Perhaps find a higher bidder?"

"We're paying him thirty million rubles, this to a man who just hours ago learned that he wouldn't be paid half the money he was promised while working on the island for three years."

Gromov paced around for a moment.

"So, what you're saying is that he's properly incentivized?"

"That's exactly what I'm saying. I have no doubt that he'll bring the package to us." Berezin paused a beat. "I'm just hoping he gets here ahead of the storm brewing off the coast."

"Is that going to be a problem?"

"It could be if it's too much to prevent our ship from arriving."

"Notify me the moment you have the seeds in your possession," Gromov said before hanging up.

Gromov walked outside and looked upward at the blue sky. He only hoped it looked the same over Svalbard.

CHAPTER 11

Grumant, Svalbard

YOLKOV BOUNCED ALONG the snow path just outside of Grumant, an abandoned Russian mining community about thirty kilometers west of Longyearbyen. Even though he knew he was clear of the Sysselmannen, he still checked over his shoulder periodically. Earning thirty million rubles for the op just seemed too easy. His wife would be upset that she hadn't heard from him during their regularly scheduled meetings. But she'd get over it when she saw the money.

The money and the expectation of seeing his family kept Yolkov going. Not that it was difficult skimming across the Arctic snow. He'd been in far more precarious situations, ones where his life was truly in danger. But this? This was a joy ride with the world's most valuable cargo.

It even got him thinking about how much money he might make if he sold the corn back to the U.S. If the seeds he'd secured in his snowmobile were important enough for the Russians to pay him thirty million rubles just to bring it to them, it'd surely fetch a higher price on the open market or even the black market. It was a thought that rattled around in his head and didn't readily go away. He loved his country, but he couldn't shake the manner in which he was fired, the way in which he was discharged. It was the narrative the Army spun, but he knew better. It was to save face in the international community. Russian brass couldn't really feel that way about him, could they? After all, why would they request his help on such a vital mission if they didn't?

The answers were obvious: Yolkov was discharged to save face globally, but Russia still respected him. And for that reason, he couldn't betray them. Not without just cause. It was his chance to not only make a significant amount of money—and maybe even a way back to the job he so loved. Or maybe a new one. Yolkov struggled to make sense of it all as he sped toward Grumant.

When Yolkov finally arrived in Grumant, he pulled over into one of the sheds on the eastern outskirts of the village. The statue of Stalin was visible, an ever-present reminder of the past glory that Russia once held. However, the stark dormitory housing units painted bland versions of white and pale orange that flanked Stalin also served as a touchstone to a bygone era. The glory was worth remembering; the oppression and dilapidated living conditions and depressed economy weren't. Yolkov decided the shed was the best place to both hide his snowmobile and enable him to easily climb higher in order to obtain a stronger cell signal. He scrambled up a perimeter wall surrounding the shed and checked his phone. Full coverage.

Yolkov smiled.

Stupid Americans.

With a NASA research station on Svalbard, the Americans brought all their technology with them when they constructed a facility there, which benefitted Yolkov momentarily. He watched his bars reach full strength and connected to a network that had the power of LTE. The island had been one of the most technologically advanced in the world since the 1980s when the cold war was in full swing. Since it ended, a simple cell tower might have been what Russia needed to push the balance of power to its side.

The phone rang three times before Berezin answered.

"Where are you?" Berezin asked.

"I'm almost there. I needed to take a break. I'm in Grumant, but I'll be there soon."

"Good. I've been trying to reach you for the past half hour. Don't you ever answer your phone during an op?"

"I'm sorry, but it's not exactly easy to answer my phone while operating a snowmobile."

"You should make it easier."

Yolkov grunted. "You can come do this yourself if you like."

"Forget it. But listen carefully. Our plans have changed."

"Changed?"

"Yes, a storm has moved in, making it far more dangerous for our sub to reach the port here. Barentsburg is no longer a viable drop off location."

"What am I supposed to do with this seed? There's no doubt the Sysselmannen is tracking me."

"You saw her?"

"I had to elude her to escape the vault, though I haven't seen any sign of her since. But I'm confident she's trying to track me now."

"In that case, we can't risk her catching you."

Yolkov picked up a rock resting on the roof and heaved it as far as he could.

"Can't you come and pick me up in the helicopter?

That'd make it much easier," Yolkov said.

"The winds are too high. It's too risky. Besides, that's exactly where the Sysselmannen will be looking for you."

"So, what am I supposed to do?"

"I'll direct our sub to meet you at the point between Torell land and Serkapp land, right off the Storfjorden on the southeastern side of the island. Do you think you can find your way there?"

"I've been there before."

"Good. We'll await your arrival."

"And what if I don't make it there?"

"You want the thirty million rubles, don't you?" Berezin said.

"I'll see you there."

Yolkov hung up and exhaled. He wasn't sure if he could navigate safely across the treacherous island, but he was going to try.

Anything for Russia?

Anything for thirty million rubles.

CHAPTER 12

Washington, D.C.

SENATOR POWELL NEEDED TO THINK, something he did best while running along the streets of the capital. He'd done enough sitting and talking and watching and waiting—and it was pushing him to the brink of insanity. Getting outside might help him clear his mind and figure out a path forward, a path leading to nobility and nowhere else.

Powell understood that the end of his time in Washington had been expedited. Once the full scope of this carefully devised and executed plot came to bear, the fickle American people would be calling for his head. A growing number of people already viewed Fenestra with disdain. In a few days, an entire nation would join them. Powell already imagined the ads running with his face slapped next to a failing cornfield and the words "Fenestra" plastered across the screen. It's what he would do if he were running against an opponent who held such an indefensible position.

The weekend was fast approaching, which gave Powell equal feelings of despair and hope. With two more days to get worked up before Monday, the mood of the country could swing angry and violent, even more so than it already had. People could spend Saturday and Sunday stewing over another government failure to protect its citizens. He even imagined some angry citizen—or perhaps even a whole mob of them—snapping and mounting an attack inside the Capitol Building.

But the next two days also gave him reason to think positively. With the markets closed for two days, stocks wouldn't crash any further—and perhaps it'd give everyone time to calm down and assuage some of their fears. It wasn't going to be the end of the world, but just another event that would change the way Americans lived, along with the rest of the world. It wouldn't be as visually striking as 9/11, but far more people would die by the time the situation was rectified . . . if it was ever rectified.

In order to launch a campaign that would stem the tide of public opinion and even shift it back into his favor, Powell needed to hear that James Flynn had taken possession of the seeds. So far, his phone hadn't rung.

Powell wondered if Flynn could even reach him.

Cell phone battery life is atrocious in the cold. Maybe he has the seeds but his battery is dead.

The scenarios in Powell's head didn't stop there.

Maybe he's trapped or got caught in one of those nasty Arctic storms. A wild animal could've attacked him. Or he fell through the ice.

Powell tightened the laces on his shoes and called Osborne at the CIA once more just to see if Flynn had called his former handler first.

"I haven't heard anything, Senator," Osborne said. "You can rest assured that the moment I hear from him, I'm going to call you."

"I appreciate that. I'm looking forward to your call. And

if for some reason I don't answer, please leave a message and let me know what's going down."

"It'll be my pleasure, Senator."

Powell hung up and started stretching. He had a place in Georgetown located near his favorite running haunt, Dumbarton Oaks Park. His golden retriever, Roosevelt, looked up at Powell longingly. Most of the time, he would take Roosevelt with him. But Powell didn't want any distractions.

"Not today, boy," Powell said as he rubbed the dog's head and gave him a quick scratch behind the ears.

Slipping in a pair of earbuds, Powell broke into a light jog along the sidewalk in front of his house. His initial intentions were never anything more than to escape the noise clanging away on his phone and television. Radio, newspapers, websites—it didn't matter the medium because the media was pursuing this story with all the fervency of a White House sex scandal.

For the first few minutes of his run, Powell experienced a pleasurable dissolution from the worries eating at him. But it didn't last long before the thoughts crept back in.

Powell grew angrier with each step, such a gradual increase that he'd hardly noticed his lightning pace. He was mad at Fenestra for breaking their trust with the FDA and inserting terminator genes into their corn seeds. He was upset at himself for trusting a company that had a history of lying. He was livid when he considered how this one event would derail his chances of serving for a long time on Capitol Hill. But nothing worked up Powell like the thought of the Russians regaining world power status while the U.S. was brushed aside like a second world country.

As he was about to turn into a park, a stretch limo pulled up next to him and screeched to a halt.

Powell continued running, ignoring the vehicle.

"Senator Powell," a man called.

Powell kept his head down.

"Senator Powell," the man shouted.

Powell stopped, took his earbuds out, and looked at the man standing next to the car.

"Coy Monroe," Powell said as he approached the Fenestra spokesperson whose face had become almost synonymous with the brand itself. "What brings you out here today?"

Monroe laughed. "I love to stalk runners in the city?"

"Are you asking me or telling me—because either way, I'm not buying it."

Monroe gestured toward his car. "We have much to discuss."

CHAPTER 13

Saturday, April 28
Longyearbyen, Svalbard

FLYNN SQUINTED AS HE CHECKED his watch and looked skyward. Is it really 2:00 a.m.? It looked like a late afternoon day based on the angle of the sun. But based on how his body felt, Flynn would've guessed a time closer to nine in the morning after he'd stayed up all night.

After the brazen thief disappeared with all the U.S. corn seed, Flynn and Larsen joined Knudsen and the vault director at the Sysselmannen's headquarters to discuss a strategy. The immediate plan was to have the Sysselmannen and one of her deputies venture out in the helicopter and see if they could find him. Even on a snowmobile, Knudsen concluded that the thief couldn't have escaped too far away.

Flynn, obliging the Longyearbyen custom of removing his shoes before entering any public building, jammed his feet into a pair of complementary slippers in the foyer of the Sysselmannen's headquarters. He stayed at the office with Larsen and listened to the activities on the radio. However, the search mission ended prematurely due to high winds that swept across the island around 1:00 a.m. Once Knudsen landed on the helipad and returned to the office,

Flynn proposed they go after the thief on snowmobiles.

"I'm afraid it might be a fruitless mission," she said in response to his proposal.

"What makes you think that?" Flynn asked.

"He could be anywhere by now. For all we know, he could be at sea."

Flynn sighed. "Isn't there a way to tell what ships are approaching Svalbard?"

"We know when something is coming down the Isfjorden, but if he transferred the seeds to another vehicle anywhere else, I'm afraid we have no way of knowing."

"Well, we can't just sit here and do nothing, can we?"

The Sysselmannen poured herself a cup of coffee.

"We'll go after him on the ground. I'm sure he's headed to Barentsburg if he isn't there already," she said.

"So, you're confident that he's Russian?" Flynn asked.

"Are you confident that he isn't?"

"Great. What are we waiting for then?" Flynn said as he snapped his fingers, eager to engage the man responsible for carrying out potentially the most devastating heist to American interests in the history of the country.

Knudsen looked at Larsen. "You up for this?"

"I'm always up for an adventure," he answered.

"Let's go. I've got two snowmobiles fueled up and ready to ride," she said, gesturing in the direction of the door.

Flynn didn't wait for another gesture or invitation, shoving his chair aside and storming toward the exit.

"Don't forget your shoes," Knudsen said to Flynn.

He hustled to put on his snow boots before shuffling across the ice toward the Sysselmannen's garage. With the garage door rolled up, the Sysselmannen shoved go-bags into the storage unit in each snowmobile.

"How long do you think we'll be out there?" Flynn asked.

She shrugged. "A day or two, maybe more. It depends on what we're up against."

"You think it'll take that long?" Flynn asked, stunned by Knudsen's assessment.

"Whoever did this is experienced, not some man who commits—how do you Americans say it?—smash and grab thefts?"

"So you're suggesting that it won't be easy?"

She opened the lid to one of the first aid kits, checking the contents inside.

"It might be the most difficult mission you've ever been on."

"I doubt that," Flynn said as he wagged his index finger at her. "I did work for the CIA at one time."

"If you think you're going to impress me by telling me that you were a spy in the past, you're going to be disappointed," she said. "There's more to surviving in the Arctic than eavesdropping and trying to bed beautiful women. James Bond wouldn't last ten minutes outside the city limits."

"I will agree with you about that," Flynn said. "Bond is little more than a figment of Ian Fleming's imagination."

She continued rifling through their supplies.

"Yet every American man I've ever met admires the fictional character."

Flynn furrowed his brow. "Is that your standard ice breaker question?"

"Shaken, not stirred," Larsen chimed in with Bond's famous catchphrase.

"There will be no martinis where we're going," Knudsen said as she straddled the seat. "Mr. Flynn, you ride tandem with me."

Flynn cracked a wry smile. "Are you always so forward with your guests?"

She let out an exasperated breath. "Get on, will you? We're losing time."

Larsen climbed onto the empty snowmobile, while Flynn jumped onto the seat behind Knudsen.

She revved the engine and eased off the clutch, jerking Flynn forward before he leaned backward and nearly fell off the seat.

"You're going to have to hang onto me," she said. "Or are you too macho to put your hands around a woman?"

Flynn obeyed and smiled to himself. He always enjoyed bantering with a quick-witted woman, though he may have met his match with Knudsen.

They rolled along for the next two hours, flying across a well-worn path heading west out of Longyearbyen. Once they reached Grumant, she signaled to Larsen to kill the engines.

"Is this the most likely safehouse location?" Flynn asked, climbing off the seat to stretch his legs.

"Nothing here could remotely be considered a safe-house, but this is certainly where I'd go. It'd be easy to hide here since all of these buildings are abandoned and tourists come through here every day to catch a glimpse at how life in the former Soviet Union was—or still is in some places."

Flynn grunted and grabbed a rifle, trudging forward through the snow.

"Let's get started. We're going to check every building, aren't we?" he asked.

"At this point, we don't have much choice," Knudsen answered.

Flynn let out his frustration by kicking in stubborn

doors, knocking a few of them off their hinges. Some of the rooms he entered appeared as if someone had fled at a moment's notice. A set table here, a stack of clean dishes there. The frigid conditions kept plenty of things just as it had been at one time when the village was bustling with life. But the harsh winters had also taken a toll on others. Roofs were blown off some buildings, rotting wood littered around the small city's main thoroughfare. Unlike most abandoned towns in the rest of the world, graffiti was noticeably absent. It was a paradox unlike any other Flynn had ever seen: A town awaiting the return of its inhabitants in some areas, while never expecting anyone in others.

They spent about an hour clearing five buildings but hadn't seen any signs of the thief anywhere.

Flynn climbed to the third floor of a building and began working through it systematically with Larsen and Knudsen.

"How did these miners live like this?" Flynn asked.

"Have you ever been to Russia?" Larsen replied. "It's all a matter of perspective."

"I've been to Russia, but I've never seen anything quite like this."

Knudsen put her finger to her lips in the hallway.

"Ssshhh."

She motioned down the hall.

Flynn and Larsen crept with her toward a noise at the end of the hallway. The pinging of a metal pan echoed, the wind whistling through the porous walls.

Knudsen reached the room where the noise appeared to be coming from and raced inside, gun drawn. Flynn leaned against the wall and waited, only to be disappointed when a fox scrambled past him.

"Not what I was hoping for," Knudsen said once she returned to the hall.

"Are you sure he's here?" Flynn asked.

"There are only so many places he can go, but it's definitely worth continuing our investigation."

Knudsen's phone then rang.

"What is it?" she said.

Flynn watched her nod a few times and furrow her brow.

"We're on our way," she said.

"What is it?" Flynn asked.

"Vilhelm Madsen just called to report that he saw our thief breaking inside the Longyearbyen Kennel and trying to assemble a team of dogs."

Flynn threw his head back, looking straight up at the ceiling.

"Isn't he the town drunk?"

"He's annoying and crazy, but he's not a drunk," Knudsen said. "I trust him. We need to get back so we stand a chance of catching him."

"And how are we going to do that?" Flynn asked.

"I work for an outfitter with better huskies than anyone will ever find at the Longyearbyen Kennel, trust me," Larsen said. "Sires of Iditarod winners. If we move quickly enough, we'll be able to catch him."

"We're not going to use snowmobiles?" Flynn said.

"There's only one reason he'd double back to get a team of dogs—he's going somewhere that requires more fuel than a snowmobile can handle," Knudsen said.

Larsen nodded. "He's headed south."

CHAPTER 14

Omsk, Russia

GROMOV HARDLY SLEPT the night before, awaiting a phone call that assured him everything was taken care of. But that call never came. First one bottle of wine, then two, neither of which helped calm his nerves. He eventually switched to vodka, which led to him standing on his veranda and cursing at people floating along the river.

"Yury, you should go lie down," Irina said, gently rubbing his back. "You need more sleep."

"How can I sleep when I do not have the information I requested?" he said before grunting. "No one is telling me anything."

"Just give them time, dear. You will know soon enough. Not everything happens when you snap your fingers."

Gromov downed another shot of vodka.

"It should."

Irina returned inside, while Gromov found another kayaker to scream at. This time, Gromov hurled the empty vodka bottle into the river to punctuate his rant.

His phone rang and he fumbled with it in an attempt to answer. It dropped onto the ground before he bent over and picked it up.

"Please tell me some good news," Gromov said.

"Father, it is fantastic news," answered his son, Vladimir.

"What is it?"

"We just received a stack of orders for new combines and harvesters. So much so that we need to increase production."

Gromov furrowed his brow. "How many?"

"I don't know the exact numbers yet, but it's going to require a capital outlay of two billion rubles."

"Two billion rubles? Where are these orders coming from?"

"All over. Apparently, many of the other companies who have diversified and also produce corn planters and harvesters can't meet the demand due to fiscal problems. But I know we have the capital to proceed, correct?"

Gromov affirmed his son's suppositions, yet didn't want to approve the project.

"If I were to approve this, it would put us in a risky financial situation," Gromov said. "We don't have much more money than that in reserves."

"So, we get a loan?"

Gromov laughed. "Have you seen the markets lately? All the uncertainty in America over its corn crops is driving the markets into chaos."

"I've seen it—and I know that's why we're getting so many orders. Farmers realize that corn is no longer the best cash crop. Now, the money is on wheat."

"Perhaps for now, which is why we're getting inundated with orders. But we still must be smart."

"Then I recommend we get a loan for a portion of the first orders and repay it quickly," Vladimir said. "We can fund the remaining portion with the amount we make off the sales of the first few orders. It will enable us to maintain a healthy solvency while funding expansion. It's brilliant."

"Let me think about it. I'm still not sure any bank will be able to loan us the money at this point. And I don't want to commit all our reserves to anything until I know what's going to happen with the U.S. corn."

"And how are you going to find out about that?" Vladimir asked, the sarcasm in his voice showing.

"I have my ways. Just wait until I get more information before you do anything. I want to be sure."

***

VLADIMIR LOATHED HIS FATHER'S CAUTIOUS approach to expanding the business. If it were up to him, Gromov Global would actually be global. It would supplant every other U.S. and European manufacturer of agricultural equipment and machinery in the world.

He called his company accountant to get an exact figure on the cash reserves the company held. It was just enough to fund the expansion.

Father will understand.

He decided to take action on the next business day, action his father was too scared to take.

CHAPTER 15

Somewhere in Svalbard

YOLKOV DROVE HIS TEAM of huskies hard toward the south. Fighting sleep depravation and hunger pangs, he pressed on. He needed the rest but couldn't afford to stop. With all the resources at the Sysselmannen's disposal, she could be right behind him.

But every time he looked over his shoulder, she wasn't there.

No whine of the snowmobiles. No gyrating blades beating the air.

The only sounds he heard were that of panting dogs and blowing wind along with the constant swish of two runners slicing through the slushy snow. It was as quiet as things had been for Yolkov in quite some time. Quiet enough for him to think.

He glanced at the horizon and noticed the dark clouds bearing down on him, creating a formidable obstacle in his path. But it was still a ways off. Until the man versus nature showdown occurred, he preferred to enjoy the moment of solitude.

A piece of Yolkov died when the Spetsnaz dismissed him from their ranks several years back. Outsmarting his opponents gave him a sense of satisfaction that he'd never been able to find anywhere else—and it certainly wasn't something he ever found at the mine. The exhilaration of successfully utilizing his physical skills and observation skills created a true tactician like the Russians hadn't seen in a while. His expertise in munitions had less to do with his training and more to do with his obsession of how explosives worked. Despite all his special talents, killing people was at the top of the list.

It had been so long since he'd taken another person's life that he felt a twinge of guilt when he snapped the neck of the man assigned to guard the Longyearbyen Kennel. It wasn't out of anger or hatred—it never was when he killed another person. It was out of necessity. And more often than not when he served in the Spetsnaz, he killed out of duty. The mission had to be completed. However, there were always exceptions, the kind of exceptions that cost Yolkov his post with the Russian special forces. But he didn't like to think about it.

When Yolkov faced a tremendous challenge, he liked to think about his son Boris. Instead of dwelling on the odds, Yolkov considered the reasons why he needed to act with precision and focus. Aside from the simple fact that he always wanted to complete his mission alive, he wanted to be alive for someone. Sometimes he thought about his wife, but mostly it was about Boris. And all of Yolkov's endeavors in the Spetsnaz were about creating a better life—a better world—for his son. No matter how dark the days in Russia seemed, Yolkov believed they could be better.

He didn't know enough about the specifics of his mission to know exactly how it would make life in Russia better, but he just knew it would. Any opportunity to stick it to the Americans and he was in. Even if it seemed as benign as something like corn seeds.

Yolkov watched the plastic blue barrel tethered to his sled. It shifted slightly back and forth as the dogs mushed along. Inside the barrel, a slop mixture sloshed around. Yolkov was getting so hungry that he contemplated joining the dogs whenever he stopped.

He glanced up at the horizon and concluded that it would be sooner rather than later. The storm clouds were approaching fast. Without delay, he needed to find a place to put down for a few hours and let the dogs rest.

Just ahead he spied a good location. Up against the side of a mountain face was a crevice. Yolkov figured it could shield them from the wind and get them out of the open where it might be easier for the Sysselmannen to see him, especially if she took to the air. An aerial reconnaissance approach wasn't likely given the storm winds, but anything that made it more difficult for his pursuers to see him was vital at this point.

He dismounted and anchored the dogs down for a spell before feeding them. A few minutes later, he set up a perimeter alarm and pitched his tent. He lay down, gun across his chest.

The wind started to howl, stirring up the dogs. They joined together in a cacophonous chorus, making it nearly impossible for Yolkov to sleep. Resisting as long as he could, he finally poked his head outside to see if there was imminent danger.

Despite the daylight, the storm's fierce wind nearly created a whiteout condition.

Still kneeling at the front of his tent, Yolkov felt the stakes starting to give way. He zipped the tent up and dove back down.

Again lying on his back, Yolkov fingered the trigger on his gun and closed his eyes.

Anything for Boris.

CHAPTER 16

Longyearbyen, Svalbard

FLYNN STRUGGLED TO HEAR Larsen shouting orders over the soulful howls from the two husky teams staked into the ground but itching to bound across the fresh Arctic snow. The temperature dropped and a light snow fell as they returned to Longyearbyen from Grumant, creating optimum conditions for running a team. Flynn dug his heels onto the brakes, though he was still unable to keep the sled from moving. The dogs dragged him a couple of meters before Larsen hustled over and wrapped the team's snub line around a fence post.

"That ought to hold them for a few more minutes," Larsen said, pulling the line taut.

"I'm afraid I'm doing more harm than good right now," Flynn said.

"You're good," Larsen answered as he finished preparations on the sled. "These dogs are just ready to run."

"I can't believe how strong they are."

"Frances and Selma there are both offspring of London, who was on a team that won the Iditarod one year."

"How much longer before we get going?" Flynn asked.

Larsen looked over his shoulder and winked at Flynn.

"We'd already be mushing if you could keep the dogs still."

Flynn broke into a smile as he turned in the direction of Knudsen, who had just finished hooking the last dog's tug line onto the team's tow line.

She flashed Flynn the thumbs-up sign.

"Ready?" she shouted to Larsen.

He nodded.

Larsen nudged Flynn off the brakes and told him to ride with Knudsen. Larsen's sled held all the food and equipment.

Flynn stopped and gaped at the stack of food and equipment on the sled.

"How long do you think we're going to be gone?" he asked.

"It's Svalbard," Larsen said. "What do you Americans say? Plan for the worst and hope for the best?"

Flynn looked southward and sighed. The lack of sleep and unfamiliarity with the terrain left him feeling unprepared for what lie ahead. Not to mention he'd never been on a dog sled before.

Larsen patted Flynn on the shoulder.

"Don't worry, mate. We'll catch him."

Flynn settled into his seat on the sled, while Knudsen stood on the runners behind him. Larsen yanked their anchor loose and attached it to their sled and signaled for Knudsen to mush.

The dogs pulled with such force that Flynn thought he was going to suffer from mild whiplash symptoms. He looked over his shoulder at Larsen, who'd also pulled his anchor out of the ground and was mushing right behind them.

They raced past a few mines and the NASA research station perched atop a ridge before entering the island's vast wilderness area. Flynn relaxed and took in the scenery, almost forgetting for a moment that he was in pursuit of seeds that would dictate the future for millions of people all across the globe. And given the surroundings, it was easy to get lost in a place that felt otherworldly.

As they plunged farther south, Flynn took in the majestic mountains flanking them on both sides. In front of them, snow danced across their path, pushed by a gusting wind. In the distance, Flynn watched a herd of reindeer digging beneath the snow for something to graze on.

After a few more minutes without conversation, Flynn spoke, too curious not to inquire about the island's first woman Sysselmannen.

"So, what brought you out to the hinterlands?" Flynn asked over his shoulder.

"You're looking at it," Knudsen said. "This and my husband."

"Your husband?" Flynn asked, certain that he never noticed a ring on her finger, though he wasn't sure the custom of wearing a wedding band was as widespread in this part of the world.

"Ex-husband now. He was awarded a job on Svalbard running a mine. I was in Tromso at the time, working as a deputy sheriff. We made it work for a while, as he commuted back on the short flight every weekend. But we had a two-year-old son at the time, and we needed to be together. I begged him to quit, but he told me he couldn't because we needed the money and it was more than he could make anywhere on the mainland. Then a post in Longyearbyen opened up for the Sysselmannen, so I applied and was selected."

"How long ago was that?"

"Eight years now."

"So, you have a ten-year-old? Even with your husband here, that must still be challenging juggling everything."

Knudsen didn't say a word. She was so quiet that Flynn wondered if she hadn't fallen off the sled. He peeked over his shoulder to see she was still firmly affixed on the sled, face stoic, hands tightly gripping the reins.

"Is your husband still working here?" Flynn finally said.

"Ex-husband. And, yes, he works in Sveagruva at the mine there."

"Are you always this warm and friendly?"

"Are you always this nosy?" she snapped.

"No, I—I just thought I'd make some polite conversation during our journey."

"Polite conversation does not involve probing questions about my family."

"I'm sorry. I wasn't trying to be rude. I was just—I was just—"

"You were just being nosy. Stop it."

Shamed into silence, Flynn remained quiet for another fifteen minutes before he spoke again.

"How do you know he's going this way?"

"It's the only way that makes sense. He wouldn't need a team of huskies if he were heading straight east. And the only logical place he'd be headed to hand off his seeds would be the southern part of the island—and this is the only way through."

"Fair enough," Flynn said.

The ravine wound to the right and eventually presented a diverging path.

"Which way now?" Flynn asked.

Knudsen shrugged and waited for Larsen, who a few seconds later pulled up next to them.

"Any ideas?" she said to Larsen as she gestured toward the two paths.

"The one on the left makes the most sense because it will put them closer to the sea—and I'd be willing to bet anything that he's trying to get the seeds to a ship or sub."

She nodded. "What else would he be doing with them? He's certainly not going to plant them here."

Flynn listened intently before he turned to the left and noticed a small building in the distance.

"What's that up there?" Flynn asked, pointing in the direction of the structure.

"That's the Sveagruva mine," Larsen said.

"It's just a couple of kilometers. It's not that far out of the way," Flynn said. "We should go ask if anyone has seen anything."

"I'm not sure that's a good idea," Knudsen said.

"Why?" Flynn asked. "All it would take would be one wrong guess before we'd be another day behind him and he'd already have handed off the seeds. Our opportunity would be gone. That's not something we can let happen."

"We don't need to go to Sveagruva," she protested.

"Why are you so adamant about this? It won't take us that long to scoot over there."

"Because my ex-husband works there, damnit! Now stop prying and keep quiet."

Flynn looked to Larsen for sympathy. He simply shrugged.

"Just keep going in silence," Larsen said. "We'll figure it out."

"We don't have much time to do that," Knudsen snapped. "Besides, we need to make camp for tonight. There's a big storm cloud moving this way. We might all be a little less annoyed with a good night's sleep."

"Nothing annoys me more than being so close to the answer but not being able to ask someone for it," Flynn said.

Knudsen slapped Flynn in the back of the head.

"We're not going to the mines—and that's the end of that."

The hum of a snowmobile in the direction of Sveagruva arrested the trio's attention. Knudsen jammed on the brakes, halting her team, while Larsen followed suit.

Flynn watched the snowmobile speed closer to their location.

"Do you know who that is?" he asked.

She nodded. "It's my ex-husband."

"The same man you didn't want to talk to? Yet now you're stopping?"

"I don't want to talk to him," she said through her teeth. "But I am the Sysselmannen, and I'm sure he has a legitimate reason for coming out to meet us. I can't ignore my duties to protect this island."

Flynn shook his head. "I know exes don't always get along, but you have a special kind of hate for him. Was he abusive? Does he mistreat your son?"

Jaw set with eyes narrowed, Knudsen held her gaze on the approaching vehicle.

"You journalist types are all alike. I know you're never going to stop asking until I tell you," she said.

Flynn's face fell. "Look, I'm sorry. I just—"

"He killed our son."

CHAPTER 17

YOLKOV AWOKE TO THE HOWLS from one of the huskies. In his desperation to set up a shelter, he'd forgotten to double check the tow line and make sure they were all secure. He poked his head out of the tent and saw another miscue induced by his hastiness: He had left the lid off the feeding barrel. The smell had attracted a small herd of reindeer, which sauntered toward his camp. But he doubted they were the only animals to catch the aroma of easy food wafting across the tundra. He needed to act quickly.

After hurrying to put on his boots and coat, Yolkov covered the barrel of slop before searching for the prodigal husky. On a small ridge about twenty meters above Yolkov's camp, the young pup threw her head back and unleashed another drawn out cry. After she finished, she walked to the edge and glared down at Yolkov.

Yolkov shuddered. It was almost as if the dog knew she and the rest of the team had been coopted for a nefarious expedition.

Scrambling up the gentle sloping incline toward the ridge, Yolkov ventured out onto the ledge near the dog.

Yolkov gingerly tapped the surface with his foot, refusing to put the full weight of his body on any portion of the ground until he'd tested it with increasing degrees of pressure. Once he felt satisfied to take a step, he would, inching closer to the animal.

"Come on, girl," Yolkov said.

The husky barked several times before taking a cautious step forward.

"That's right. Come here."

Another step.

"That's it. Keep moving."

The dog edged to within an arm's length of Yolkov. He then lunged for the dog, but she was too quick, darting around him and down the slope.

Yolkov spun around to watch her race past the rest of the team, riling them up. They all howled, jerking hard on their line.

As he watched the scene unfold, Yolkov hustled down the incline, his eyes darting between the slippery terrain in front of him and the team. With almost orchestrated movement, the dogs began to loosen the anchor. Yolkov watched it loosen from the ice with each concerted tug on the line.

Once he reached the level surface, he sprinted toward the dogs, stomping on the anchor to re-secure it. Using his heel to depress it farther into the ice, Yolkov breathed a short sigh before turning his attention back to the wayward husky. Losing one dog on the line wouldn't devastate the team, but it certainly would slow him down.

Yolkov wrapped his frigid hand around the gun, clutching it tight. Jamming his other hand into his pocket, he trudged out into the open where the dog had stopped fifty meters away. With paws stretched out in front of her, she pressed her belly to the ice almost as if she were shirking back from something.

The wind had kicked up once Yolkov stepped out from behind the nook that had been shielding him from the full force of the storm. With snow blowing sideways, he struggled to see anything beyond the dog.

Yolkov stopped for a moment to look back north.

Still no company.

Yolkov recalled the familiar feeling of being close to completing an assignment. The satisfaction of success would soon be his to revel in. It also meant he would return home soon. He could almost feel Boris' wiry frame in his arms and smell the top of his head. It wouldn't be long. While this endeavor hadn't been easy by any measure, it had been relatively devoid of imminent danger.

Until that moment.

Yolkov looked up to see a polar bear prowling nearby. It didn't appear as imposing as other beasts Yolkov had seen. The emaciated animal looked more ill than fierce, though Yolkov knew a thin bear was the most dangerous type of polar bear on the island. Hungry bears would settle on any source of meat they could find—and there were two of them within twenty meters.

Yolkov halted before slowly walking backward. He had a gun big enough to kill the polar bear if necessary, but he didn't want to verify the gunmaker's claim. Preferring to take the manufacturer's word for it, Yolkov increased the distance between him and the bear until he reached the camp.

As the behemoth animal circled the dog, it shot angry

glances at her.

However, the dog didn't move.

Perhaps paralyzed by fear, she remained still, stomach pressed to the ground.

The team of dogs started to howl, which resulted in the polar bear shifting from a plodding gait to a light jog. Yolkov could tell the dogs were doing nothing but irritating the beast.

Acting quickly, he spooned out bowls of slop for the dogs, bringing their howling to an end. He turned his attention back to the dog, who still hadn't moved.

The polar bear was within a few meters, though it had slowed its pace.

Come on, girl. Get out of there.

Once the polar bear pounced, the dog darted to the side and dashed in a westerly direction, away from Yolkov and the rest of the team. With the polar bear in pursuit, Yolkov pulled out a pair of binoculars and watched the action, but not before glancing toward the horizon to see another storm heading in his direction.

Across the way, the dog managed to escape momentarily in the open, but once she reached an icy mountain face, she struggled to find her footing.

When the polar bear reached her, the dog was still scratching at the ice, trying to get traction. But she failed.

Yolkov dropped his binoculars unable to watch and winced when a high-pitched yelp reached his ears.

Whenever this weather relents, guess I'll have to make do with seven dogs.

CHAPTER 18

Sveagruva, Svalbard

FLYNN RUBBED HIS EYES and checked his watch. With the never-setting sun hovering on the horizon, he learned quickly that the instincts about time he'd cultivated in the rest of the world didn't apply in the Arctic. It was 4:00 a.m. He'd managed to get six solid hours of sleep, though his body cried out for more. He slept soundly thanks to the steady rhythms of the wind whipping snow against the side of the Sveagruva mining shelter.

He lay there for a moment going over in his mind the tense conversation between Knudsen and her husband, Ragnar.

The way that Knudsen tersely described her ex-husband, Flynn thought the man would look and act much more differently than he did. Instead of an abrasive man with little thought for others, Flynn found him to be quite the opposite.

When Ragnar had reached them on his snowmobile, he climbed off and introduced himself, shaking Flynn's hand and patting him on the back in a collegial manner. Knudsen directed the conversation toward business almost immediately, dispensing with all polite pleasantries. To Flynn, it appeared as if she wanted this brief meeting to occur like she wanted a hole in her knee cap.

Ragnar warned them about a storm that was fast approaching and urged them to seek cover in Sveagruva until it passed.

"Have you seen anyone mushing lately?" Flynn asked.

"Yesterday, I saw a man headed due south," Ragnar said. "I can't say where he was going, but he was driving his team hard." He studied all three faces for a moment. "What's going on?"

Knudsen seethed. "It's none of your—"

"Someone has stolen the U.S. corn seeds from the vault—and it's extremely important that we retrieve them," Flynn said.

Ragnar furrowed his brow. "Someone broke into the seed vault?"

"Where have you been?" Knudsen said. "Obviously not back in Longyearbyen where this heist is the talk of the town. If you weren't so obsessed with this mine—"

"Then what? Tell me. I want to hear it from your own lips. Just say it."

Knudsen stopped and exhaled. "Never mind."

"If catching this guy is so important, I recommend waiting out the storm. It won't be over until tomorrow afternoon. You can go back out then," he told them.

He glanced at their sleds. "Though I wouldn't if I were you if he's truly headed to the southern coast."

Flynn eyed him carefully. "Why's that?"

"Because you don't have enough provisions. Those dogs will limp home. Finn, you know better than that."

"Of course I do, but I didn't account for so much bad weather."

Ragnar crossed his arms and stared down at the teams.

"You might be able to make it if you trimmed your teams back to six dogs each and lightened your load."

Flynn was no husky expert, but he wanted to learn.

"And how exactly do you intend to do that?" he asked.

"Simple. Share the food and eliminate a passenger," Ragnar said.

"I'm not leaving them." Knudsen put her hands on her hips and slowly shook her head.

"Perhaps you could fly back and meet them to restock their supplies," Ragnar offered.

"That's not necessary. We're going to catch this guy sooner rather than later—and our supplies won't matter. We'll have more than enough to make it back."

"With an additional passenger? If you think we're in that much danger of running out of supplies, I suggest you go get them and fly—"

Knudsen stopped, letting her words hang in the air. Flynn could tell she wanted to say more but couldn't—or wouldn't.

Ragnar nodded knowingly and looked down. "You may want to stay here with them, but you know I'm right. If I fly you back to Longyearbyen, you can gather all the supplies you need and take out the Sysselmannen's helicopter. Agree?"

Knudsen let out an exasperated breath and stared skyward. After a long pause, she nodded.

"OK, fine."

Ragnar turned toward Flynn and Larsen.

"You can stay at one of our overnight cabins and get some good sleep. You're going to need it for what you have ahead of you. I'll radio to one of my men and have them set you up. But whatever you do, don't leave before noon."

Flynn smiled as he recalled the exchange from the day before. He looked at his watch again: 4:05 a.m. Then he looked across the room for Larsen, who was nowhere to be found. His bed was already made, his bags restored to their proper order.

Flynn shuffled across the floor toward the bathroom to relieve himself. When he exited the room, he turned around and saw a smiling Larsen, staring him in the face and holding out a fresh cup of coffee.

"You ready to go?" Larsen asked.

"I thought Ragnar said it wasn't safe to leave until later," Flynn shot back.

"Safety is relative, but what isn't relative is how much time we have left. It's finite and shrinking by the moment."

"I'm with you. We've got to make sure those seeds never leave this island in someone else's hands." Flynn paused. "You really think we can do this in a driving storm?"

Larsen shook his head. "That's why we're not following the exact path the thief did. We're going to take a more scenic route, one that is a farther distance but shielded by mountains. I'm hoping our ability to mush on will enable us to make up any lost time, maybe even get there before he does."

"This is your territory," Flynn said. "I hope you're right."

CHAPTER 19

SENATOR POWELL CLOSED HIS EYES as he turned on the television at 10:30 on Monday morning. He slowly turned the volume up on the remote and braced for the bad news. The talking heads shouting over one another on a financial program airing on a cable news network delivered the devastating news without sugar-coating it.

"If you're growing corn in your backyard right now, you might as well be growing gold," one of the commentators said. "As if we didn't think corn could go any higher last week, it's now risen to $400 a bushel. Remember a week ago when it had risen to $5.50 and everyone was squawking about it? That feels like a distant memory now."

His partner chimed in.

"What's worse is we have no idea where the ceiling is for corn," he said. "It's used in so many different products that we don't eat, resulting in either a gold rush for substitute products or a battle royal for every stalk of corn that's currently in the ground. And let me tell you, there aren't many stalks growing right now in this great country."

The other commentator straightened a stack of papers

in front of him before continuing the miserable report as it related to U.S. interests.

"However, another crop that U.S. farmers bailed on in recent years due to its depressed price is wheat. Since that crop can serve as a quasi-substitute for corn in some cases, such as feeding livestock, its price has tripled over the past few days. And guess who holds the bulk of this wheat?"

"Oh, I don't know, Frank. Let me guess?" the other commentator said with a sarcastic tone. "Maybe it's Russia."

"Ding, ding, ding. Tell him what he's won, Bob."

Powell didn't need to hear another word, turning off the television and tossing the remote onto his desk in disgust. According to trusted advisors, the damage wasn't complete and debilitating—yet. However, it was crippling, which seemed to be the goal all along. The American economy would be forced to limp along until it managed to find a way to return to the high level of corn production the country was enjoying before this ambush attack. Though if Powell was completely honest, it wasn't an ambush.

Unexpected? Yes, but only in terms of when. For the Department of Defense, the Department of Homeland Security, and the U.S. Food and Drug Administration, this recent turn of events was anything but a surprise. They'd suspected some foreign enemy or terrorists might attempt such a strike. But the scope and precision of this particular attack was almost unforeseeable. They never anticipated anyone would be able to devastate the U.S. corn crop in such a manner.

Powell had yet to hear back about the cobbled together operation—or better yet, a prayer—taking place in the Arctic. He couldn't sit around and do nothing other than hope

SEEDS OF WAR | 109

for a positive outcome. If the plan didn't work, America wasn't just going to hell in a hand basket, but she was being delivered to the devil's front doorstep with flowers and a bottle of wine. Russia would show no mercy in the way it gleefully devoured American interests, saving only those who became complicit in the country's systematic dissolution of a once-great nation. As the developments of the past few days began to unfold, it seemed to him that the only thing left to add to the handwriting on the wall was an exclamation point to punctuate America's demise.

He called one of his aides.

"I need to speak to Fenestra's CEO right now," Powell demanded.

A few minutes later, Powell's office phone rang.

"Sir, I have Fenestra CEO Phillip Wilson on line two for you," his aide said.

Powell picked up the receiver and punched a button on the handset.

"Mr. Wilson, thank you for making the time to talk with me," Powell began.

"I didn't think I had much choice," Wilson said tersely. "You and other politicians are already pointing a serious accusatory finger at me."

"Let's put all of that aside for right now. We can't change the past and the fact that you broke your promise not to inject the terminator gene into corn seeds, otherwise we might not be having this conversation."

"If you had protected us with proper legislation, Senator, we never would've considered such an option. Besides, if you really want to point a finger, it should be at Taranto for their seed coating snafu."

"Like I said, we can't change the past. However, I'm very interested in rewriting the future. There might even be some legislative changes in it for you if you're willing to work with us."

Wilson huffed a polite laugh through his nose. "As if any of you gutless spines in Washington would dare propose a bill helpful to Fenestra that has a snowball's chance in hell of passing now."

"Mr. Wilson, sleight of hand is my specialty here in Washington. Besides, the people nor the media aren't savvy enough to comprehend the implications of certain legislative language, especially when it's tacked on to a bill everyone wants to see pushed through."

Wilson sighed. "So, let's say I agree to help. What are you looking for me to do?"

"I need you to make a public statement that you'll dedicate all your company's resources to resolving this issue and preventing a full-blown crisis from happening."

"Are you aware that due to attacks from LES—no thanks to any government law enforcement agency for sniffing out the attack—all our seed growing facilities that could make this a reality have been decimated. And Noah Barton, who claimed responsibility for this, is still on the loose. If you want to scapegoat someone, he's your guy, but you can't even catch him or any of his people."

Powell drummed his fingers on his desk. "According to intelligence reports, we're working on catching him. And last I heard, we're very close to arresting him."

"If you're looking for a political win or some way to calm the frayed nerves of the American people, I'm afraid you've come to the wrong place. There's not much I can offer in the way of hope."

Powell chuckled. "Mr. Wilson, I'm not asking you to offer actual hope. I simply want you to release a statement that you're going to be doing all you can to help."

"With all due respect, Senator, we already have a PR problem. I'd rather not give our detractors more fuel for the fire."

"Your house is already burning. What could it hurt?"

"Good day, Senator," Wilson said before hanging up.

Before Powell could hang up the receiver, his intercom buzzed.

"How'd it go, sir?" his aide asked.

"Bloody awful. We've got a mess on our hands."

"Sorry, sir. I just got a call from the White House and the president wants to speak with you in two minutes."

Powell threw his head back and sighed as he stared blankly at the ceiling.

"Scratch that. He's calling now."

Can my day get any worse?

"Good morning, Mr. President," Powell said as he answered his phone.

"There's nothing good about today. It's Monday and everything is going to shit. Can you please give me some good news? It seems like everyone is doing their best to duck my calls."

"If they are getting the kind of results I am, I know why they're avoiding you," Powell said. "I almost did it myself."

"I understand everyone is taking a political beating over this and your chances for re-election are slim, so how about you help me out here. Maybe a little quid pro quo."

"Not saying that I can, but if I can, what are you offering?"

"I just received word that Don Kramer is resigning from his post as Secretary of State at the end of the summer, and I can't think of a better candidate to replace him that you."

"Sir, I—" Powell stammered.

"I know. You don't know what to say. Hopefully, you'll say yes when I ask you. But we've got a long way to go between now and then."

"What do you want me to do, sir?"

"I want you to come up with a plan that will make the American people calm down. We need to break it to them gently that the next year or so things will be rough, but we'll get through it together."

Powell took a deep breath. "Wouldn't an address from the Oval Office accomplish that?"

"That's what I'm counting on. But I need you to lead and get me some tangible action points that I can present to the people, things that this office is already doing that will help me make that address with a some shred of integrity, even if it's the thinnest of shreds."

"I'll see what I can do."

"No, Powell, you make it happen. I'm planning on making this speech Friday night."

"Yes, sir."

"And call me the minute you hear from the former operative in the Arctic. I want to know the second we have possession of those seeds."

Powell exhaled and hung up the phone. It was already intense enough with his own political future hanging in the balance, but the stakes were raised. Another term seemed like a lost cause. He was fighting between returning to the dreaded academic world or serving as the Secretary of State.

He wrung his hands as he stood up and paced around his office for a few minutes.

Time to turn up the heat on some people.

CHAPTER 20

GROMOV TOSSED BACK A GLASS of champagne and used the back of his hand to dab the droplets eking out of the corners of his mouth. However, he still couldn't wipe the smile off his face. Giddy with excitement, he poured two glasses and held one up to his wife.

"Isn't it a little early to be celebrating?" Irina asked. "I wasn't aware that anything significant had actually happened."

Gromov handed her a glass.

"Now, dear, things are happening all the time, but you're just blissfully unaware. And I like it that way."

"So what happened this time while I was living my life and didn't notice?" she said with a smile before sipping her champagne.

"I just called my investment banker and had him buy millions of dollars worth of wheat futures."

She stared at him, unimpressed.

"And?"

He signed and rolled his eyes. "And, the market is trending upward, so I bought now in order to sell high later on. There's no telling where it's going to stop. You're looking at the president of a company that controls over half the world's wheat."

She raised an eyebrow. "And President Mirov allowed you to do this?"

He waved her off. "I don't have to get Mirov's approval for anything. Our only agreement has been fulfilled, more or less. I did my part and he did his. We worked together to lower wheat prices. Now it's time that they soar and we benefit."

"Aren't you already benefitting from the sale of your machines to all those poor farmers?"

"All those poor farmers are about to get wealthy, too, when they receive their subsidy from the government for falling in line with Mirov's incentives."

"Hmm."

Gromov eyed Irina cautiously.

"I thought you'd be more pleased than you're acting."

"I've never found pleasure in profiting off another person's loss."

Gromov moaned and pulled out a bottle of vodka.

"How do you think anyone creates wealth any more? True communism died years ago here, remember?"

"I wasn't aware that it necessitated replacement by such a cruel and unfair system."

He chugged a glass before pouring another.

"Cruel and unfair? Have you lost your mind? Nothing could be further from the truth."

"Only those with money after the breakup of the empire have succeeded in this new system. And those who had no money seem to be worse off than before."

"They're not worse off; they're better. And they know it."

She put down her glass and sank into one of the parlor chairs.

"How do you know? Have you asked them?"

"I know I'm better off—and that's all you should care about."

She looked down and rubbed her forehead with her hand.

"How did you make your money?"

He finished his glass of vodka and slammed it on the table.

"How did we get our money is more like it. And if you must know, we earned it."

"Through bribes and extortion? How very fair of you."

"Come on, Irina. It wasn't like that, and you know it."

"I know the truth, but tell yourself whatever you like if it helps you sleep at night."

He smiled. "What's going to help you sleep better at night is a plush new bed at our new beachfront home in Madeira."

She whipped her head toward him, mouth agape.

"Oh, dear, you know that's my favorite place we've ever vacationed."

Irina stood up and walked toward him, throwing her arms around him.

"You're the best."

He grinned. "So, you've changed your mind about this financial system?"

She shook her head. "No, but I can accept it."

"A few weeks in Madeira every year should help you come around."

She hugged him again and then clapped quietly.

"So, when can I see the home?"

He put his hands on her shoulders. "I'm working out all the details with my accountant later this afternoon. I decided that instead of expanding the business like Vladimir wants to do, I'd rather enjoy the fruits of our labor. I figured what's the use in working hard for all this money if you're not going to enjoy it."

"Finally," Irina said, throwing her hands in the air. "I've been waiting for you to come to this realization."

Gromov kissed her on the cheek. "All in due time, my dear."

His phone rang, interrupting their celebratory mood.

"If you'll excuse me, I need to take this call," he said.

She nodded and smiled. "Go ahead. Come find me when you're finished." Then she mouthed the words to him, in the bedroom.

He laughed and turned his attention to the phone call. It was his accountant.

"Have you got everything in order? I just broke the news to Irina about the place in Madeira. She can't wait to see it."

"You may want to hold off on that, sir."

"Why is that?"

"There seems to be a problem with your funds, or lack thereof, I should say."

"What are you talking about? We have more than enough cash on hand that I could pull out for this purchase."

"I'm afraid you don't, sir. It seems that you transferred almost your entire cash reserves this morning to begin work on another project."

"Vladimir! I'm going to kill him!"

Gromov hung up the phone and let out a string of expletives. He slumped into his chair, seething. He remembered explicitly instructing his son to wait.

I should've never given him access to the company's financials.

Gromov's phone rang again.

"Please tell me you have good news," Gromov began.

"I don't have bad news, sir, but it's not good either," said the army aide.

"Go on."

"We're still waiting on the operative to give us the seeds. But to our knowledge, he still has them in his possession."

"Don't call me again unless you have them."

"Yes, sir."

Gromov hung up and hurled his phone at the couch.

He went outside and yelled at a few kayakers before chunking a glass into the water. He felt better for a moment, but it was a fleeting emotion.

He needed to regroup—and exert control over something, anything.

He'd figure out a way to get what he wanted, one way or another.

CHAPTER 21

Svalbard

YOLKOV CLIMBED A RISE and peered through his binoculars at the Hornsundtind peak, which was due west from his location. He estimated he was about 120 kilometers away from the drop location in Sorkapp Land, which meant at least a day and a half of mushing. At a couple of degrees below 0 Celsius, the huskies struggled to run as fast. If Yolkov pushed them too hard, he risked losing another dog or two due to heat exhaustion. And at this point, that wasn't something he could afford.

Almost there. You can do it.

Yolkov was tired, both physically and mentally. The constant threat of danger was real, just as it was perceived. Mother nature along with her untamed beasts could just as easily take him out as could a sniper rifle shot from the Sysselmannen or an American operative. The farther south Yolkov travelled, the more he realized how truly exposed he was, both to the elements and anyone who wanted him stopped.

For the past couple of days, however, it was that threat of danger from a violent weather system moving across the Arctic Circle that enabled him to get this far. Mother nature wasn't partisan in targeting helpless humans. Like a raging alcoholic with a loaded gun, she took shots at everyone, unable to discern friend from foe, good from evil. She simply fired and reloaded.

But the storm that swept through the lower region of Svalbard had dissipated, leaving Yolkov with sunny skies and fresh powder. It meant he could go farther sooner, but so could those pursuing him.

Yolkov mushed along, trying to keep his mind sharp and not grow faint from the journey. He'd hardly eaten aside from a few pieces of jerky and lapping up a couple of bowls of the team's slop.

A small price to pay for thirty million rubles.

Yolkov thought about what he'd do when he returned home. He'd take his family on a long vacation, maybe Bali or somewhere on the southern coast of Spain. They'd relax on the beach, play in the sand, enjoy one another's company. It'd revitalize them all and help them reconnect after being apart for so long. More than anything, Yolkov wanted to take his son to a professional soccer match, maybe a game in Germany or Spain, maybe even Italy. Boris wouldn't care. He'd wear a stubborn grin no matter where it was, no matter what the outcome.

After a long run, Yolkov spotted a small stream gushing out of the side of a mountain and pooling on the ground below. The warmer weather combined with the sunshine likely resulted in the melt. It'd refreeze at night, but it was a treat the huskies would lap up.

Yolkov guided the team toward the water and anchored them in right by the edge. He laughed at their exuberance as they slurped up the water. Yolkov knelt down next to them and rubbed their heads. Leaving in such a rush, he hadn't had much time to build any rapport with the dogs, but he was starting to make headway with them. Even so, he feared what would happen to them. He hoped some researchers would find them before the polar bears did. He tried to shake off that thought and focus on finishing the task.

Yolkov dipped an empty water bottle into the pool and joined the huskies in gulping down the refreshing glacier water. He plopped down into the snow and closed his eyes, soaking up the suns rays on his face. That was when all the lapping stopped.

He opened his eyes and looked down at the dogs, who all had perked their ears back with heads held high. Following their lead, Yolkov leaned to his left, putting his right ear upward so he could listen.

At first he didn't hear anything, just the panting of dogs. Then he heard it. The low dull beats of helicopter blades.

He stood up and looked northward.

In the distance, he could see the Sysselmannen's chopper weaving its way back and forth across the expanse.

He didn't have much time before she'd be able to spot him—and then it was all over. Not only would he not get his thirty million rubles, but he might never see his family again.

Yolkov jerked the tow line to get the dogs' attention before scrambling to prepare to return to mushing. There was a small enclave he spotted earlier where he could hide until the helicopter moved on to another area. It was about a kilometer away, and if he hurried, he could make it before she noticed him.

Yolkov yanked up the anchor and stepped off the brake,

urging the team forward with various calls. They responded by tearing out across the snow so quickly that Yolkov almost lost his balance once the sled caught and began moving forward.

After a few seconds, Yolkov looked over his shoulder at the helicopter. It ceased its zig-zag pattern and was now making a straight line toward him.

He returned his gaze straight ahead. He only had 200 more meters until he could retreat to safety. But if the Sysselmannen set down the helicopter, it'd be a gun fight he didn't want to engage in, especially with his limited munitions. Then there was the fact that he actually respected her after their two brief interactions. Yolkov found her to be even-handed in her administration of justice when she dealt with a pair of incidents at Barentsburg. Her serious demeanor communicated to him that she wasn't someone to be messed with.

Yet Yolkov was messing with her on the grandest of scales.

Just a few more meters.

Yolkov drove the team into the enclave and waited until he felt they were sufficiently deep enough in the cavern that the Sysselmannen couldn't see them if she hadn't already. If she got out to scout the area, the dogs would surely give away their position. He quickly pulled out their bowls and dished out some food before creeping back to the entrance to see what would happen.

The thrum of the blades grew stronger, increasing in intensity with Yolkov's pounding heartbeat.

CHAPTER 22

Svalbard

FLYNN GAPED AT THE HORNSUNDTIND PEAK casting a shadow over the valley below them. Larsen decided to mush atop the mountain faces as opposed to cutting through the valley. He'd escorted plenty of researchers to the mountaintops and knew the easiest route to the top that wouldn't tax out the husky teams. Flynn and Larsen rode side by side with their sleds for much of the day, mostly in silence.

After a long period without a single word being exchanged between them, Flynn engaged Larsen in conversation.

"Do you think we'll be able to catch him?" Flynn asked.

Larsen shrugged. "It depends on what kind of obstacles he's facing. Weather, bears, exhaustion—it's hard to say at this point."

"If we're going to catch him, when do we need to see him by?"

"That's entirely dependent upon where he's dropping off the seeds. But my best guess is that he's meeting a ship at the southern tip. It'd be the easiest place for him to drop it off and avoid lingering in the area before another seafaring vessel found them."

"Do you think we're far behind?"

Larsen chuckled. "You sure are full of questions today, aren't you? You're like a little kid in the back of a car: Are we there yet?"

"I don't like entering a mission unprepared and in unfamiliar territory. I can improvise when necessary, but I feel like I'm trying to take on two hostiles at once—the thief and the island."

"That's what I'm here for. I trust my instincts with the island; you trust yours with the mission. We'll manage."

After another minute of silence, Larsen pointed at the rifle strapped to Flynn's back.

"How good of a shot are you with that?"

"Depends on the conditions, but I'd say better than most."

"Out here, the conditions will always be the worst. You can bank on that."

Flynn sighed and scanned the area for the thief. Still nothing.

"We're on our own now, you know that, right?" Larsen said. "The Sysselmannen may have gone back for a helicopter, but there's no guarantee she's going to reach us with all the storms that have been swirling in the area."

No sooner had Larsen spoken than both he and Flynn craned their necks behind them as they heard the blade beats of a helicopter in the distance.

"I'm going to go out on a limb and count on her for this mission," Flynn said with a smile.

"Don't get too cocky. She still has to land that bird. And let me tell you, it's not easy if there are high winds."

Flynn licked his index finger and stuck it in the air.

"Doesn't feel like high winds to me."

"You're not in the valley. The conditions can vary drastically, depending on your altitude on the island."

Flynn watched Knudsen maneuver back and forth across the vast expanse, sometimes nearly disappearing on the horizon.

"What is she doing?"

"She's scanning. It's how we conduct search and rescue operations out here. It's very easy to miss someone as they can vanish beneath a snow drift in a matter of seconds."

Flynn stared at the valley below.

"It's calm for the time being."

"It always looks that way up here. Everything is white. If you want to gauge conditions in the valley, you have to find some constants to serve as your guide."

Flynn picked out a rock and watched it. He seemed surprised how right Larsen was as the rock appeared to fade in and out of his vision due to the blowing snow.

"Fascinating," Flynn said. "It's still windy down there."

"And I'm not sure she could land that chopper even if she found our mystery musher."

"She'll try, won't she?"

Larsen smiled. "Don't worry. She's fearless—but cautious. No matter the consequences, she's not going to do anything stupid. She's confident enough that if she doesn't get them today, she'll get them tomorrow. If I've seen her do it once, I've seen her do it a hundred times. And she always makes the arrest."

Larsen endured a pregnant pause before continuing.

"Why? Do you fancy her or something?"

"I'm just concerned, that's all. I don't want to see her get hurt on my account."

Larsen laughed. "Believe me when I say this: If she didn't want to be here, she wouldn't."

"She's the consummate thrill seeker?"

"And so much more."

They mushed on for another half hour, watching the Sysselmannen sweep back and forth across the valley. At one point, Flynn was convinced he saw her flash the thumbs-up sign to them. But he almost all but forgot about her when he spotted another person sledding in the valley.

"Look. Down there," Flynn shouted as he pointed toward the southeast section of the valley. "Think that's him?"

Larsen pulled out his binoculars and studied the figure running the team along the eastern side of the valley.

"It's hard to say."

"This part of the island is that popular?"

"It's not, but I'm not ready to charge down into polar bear land until I'm sure it is."

Flynn scanned the area. "Polar bears are plentiful in this portion of Svalbard?"

"I wouldn't say plentiful, but I can almost guarantee you that we'll run into at least a couple once we hit the valley. But don't worry—for the most part, they stick to themselves."

"And if they don't?"

Larsen smiled and shook his head. "For a former CIA operative, you sure do spook easily."

"I'm trained to disarm and contain deadly assassins that are roughly my same size," Flynn said. "But the whole polar bear threat? That's a new one for me."

"Just don't panic. You'll be fine."

As they sped along atop the mountain, Larsen led them closer to the edge so he could get a better look at their counterpart in the valley. After a few minutes of studying him, he dropped his binoculars.

"Yep, that's him," Larsen announced. "We need to head down the mountain and join him in the valley if we're going to stand a chance at catching him."

"Lead the way," Flynn said before falling in line behind Larsen.

Over the next several minutes, they descended to the valley floor, though they still remained at least ten kilometers behind the man Larsen fingered as their target.

The Sysselmannen hovered back into the area just as the wind began to swirl around them. More loose snow drifted along the open spaces, creating a visual effect that made the ground appear to move. It also let Flynn believe they were moving faster than they actually were.

Larsen aimed to remain out of the man's line of sight as long as possible, hoping that they would never even be seen.

However, he didn't have to worry about it as he hit the brakes no more than fifty meters after they reached the valley floor.

Flynn pulled up alongside Larsen.

"What's wrong?"

Larsen put his index finger to his lips. "Ssshhh." He then pointed straight ahead.

Prowling in front of them was a polar bear.

Flynn froze, refusing to even move his lips as he asked a question.

"What do we do?"

"Stay right where you are."

Several dogs started to bark at the bear.

"Nei. Nei," Larsen said, urging the dogs to settle down. They transitioned from barking to soft growling.

"Are we just going to try and wait him out?" Flynn asked. "We don't have time for this."

"If he isn't attacking us, I'm not going to shoot him," Larsen snapped. "This is his home, not ours."

"Is there another way out of this?" Flynn said. "Maybe draw his attention away from us so we can slip past him?"

Larsen smiled. "This is most definitely your first time in the Arctic. Survival here requires patience and prepared-ness."

"And we didn't have time to fully prepare, nor can we be patient."

"Quite the conundrum, eh?"

Flynn wasn't amused.

The wind started to whip more intensely across the val-ley, reducing visibility as snow drifted past them.

"What do you make of those clouds?" Flynn pointed to the horizon.

"Would you be quiet?" Larsen said through his teeth without even glancing at Flynn. "If we're going to get past him, we have to be silent and still."

No sooner had Larsen said that than he leapt off his brakes and onto his runners and urged the dogs forward.

Flynn didn't hesitate in following the guide.

As soon as they raced past the area where the polar bear had been pacing, Flynn looked over his shoulder. The bear appeared confused and didn't chase after them.

"What are you doing?" Flynn shouted.

"If we don't find cover in a few minutes, we're going to be a buffet for that bear." Larsen pointed skyward. "Do you see those clouds?"

"That's why I was asking about them."

"They're going to kill us all if we don't find shelter and set up a perimeter alarm."

Flynn looked around, baffled by Larsen's response. They were mushing across the valley without any discernible cover in sight.

"Where are we going?"

"There's a glacial cave up ahead that'll provide some cover for us."

Flynn had already established the fact that he was a rookie when it came to Arctic exploration, but something didn't feel right to him about Larsen's idea.

"So, we're going to back into a cave with only one exit? Isn't that the epitome of backing yourself into a corner?"

Larsen bobbed his head from side to side. "How do you Americans say it? Pick your poison? We don't really have a choice at this point. We just need to get somewhere safe to avoid the storm. If the winds become too strong, we're going to be attacked if the bear feels so inclined."

"There really isn't another way?"

Larsen shook his head. "Stay close."

Flynn swallowed hard as they charged across the ice. He'd long since come to terms that he could quite possibly die at the hands of another human being while involved in such missions, but he'd never considered what it might be like to get ripped limb from limb by a hungry polar bear or simply an angry one. No matter the reason, Flynn wasn't interested in staring death in the face by one of the fiercest mammals walking across the planet. He certainly wasn't keen on backing into a tight space where he was certain that Larsen held the advantage if the bear only wanted one of them.

The wind blasted its way past him, whisking away any last layer of warmth. His face turned cold before being pelted by snow.

"How much farther?" he yelled to Larsen.

"Stay close. We're almost there."

Flynn followed Larsen's edict and stuck close. They veered toward a cave up ahead.

Looking over his shoulder back toward the valley, Flynn noticed a polar bear charging toward them with some foreign object hanging out of its mouth. He also saw Knudsen banking the Sysselmannen's helicopter northward away from them.

Flynn tightened his grip on the reins and tried not to think about all the unique ways he could die in the tundra.

CHAPTER 23

YOLKOV WATCHED THE HELICOPTER circle past his hiding spot as it skimmed the ground before leaving the area. The dogs finished eating and wasted no time in howling. With the helicopter almost out of earshot, Yolkov didn't mind the yelps. For the first time in several days, he felt like he could relax for a minute or two.

The sun flirted with setting like it did every day in the endless sunshine of summer. Yolkov had grown accustomed to this cruel fact of Arctic life, but he never liked it. If just for an hour, he wanted to see the sun vanish and night fall. In this part of the world, losing the privilege of stargazing seemed like a cruel tradeoff for twenty-four hours of daylight. Yolkov would trade endless sun just to see a sky sprinkled with twinkling stars and long brushstrokes comprised of distant galaxies—until night held fast without interruption and he'd trade stars for the sun. It was a novelty that lost its allure within the first year of his tour at the mine.

He'd told Boris about the Arctic sky and promised to one day take him to see it in person. Boris lit up whenever Yolkov talked about how the Northern Lights danced so close to the ground sometimes that he felt like he could reach out and touch them.

It was a memory—and a promise—that Yolkov held fast to. Without it, he'd plunge into a bitter cavern of ungratefulness, unable to appreciate the natural beauty around him. Yet it was the picturesque scene with its exotic landscapes and wild beasts that Yolkov so desperately wanted to escape.

He contemplated trying to strike out in the storm, finish his mission with gritty determination. But he needed to confirm that he wouldn't reach the drop location and be left exposed. The delivery needed to be swift and timely. And from where he was some forty kilometers away, he couldn't see any ships, even when he used his binoculars.

Yolkov pulled out his satellite phone from his bag and removed the phone's battery from his breast pocket. One of the most important maxims drilled into his head during his operative training was "cold kills batteries". And he endeavored to keep them insulated.

He jammed the battery into place and waited for a few seconds while the phone powered up. Then he dialed the number for Nikolai Berezin. On the fourth ring, Berezin answered.

"I trust you still have the package?" Berezin said.

"Yes, sir. I am not detained at the moment and still possess the target asset. However, I'm only about thirty kilometers from the location, and I need you to confirm that you are there."

"That's a negative, agent Yolkov," Berezin said. "Stormy seas and some mechanical issues have delayed our approach. We should arrive early tomorrow morning around 7:00 a.m. Will you be able to meet the ship at that time?"

"I'll do my best, Commander Berezin."

"I will see you tomorrow."

Yolkov hung up and disassembled the phone, returning the phone battery back to his breast pocket.

Team, it looks like we're staying here for the night, so get comfortable.

The wind whistled past the entrance to the cavern. Ice dripped with the consistency of a metronome as summer grappled with winter to release its tight grip on the island. Summer would eventually win, but winter wasn't yielding without a fight.

Yolkov set up his perimeter alarm and took shelter in a small pup tent he'd packed. He could've skipped it and slept in nothing but a sleeping bag. But he wanted some extra level of warning in case a polar bear crashed into his campsite and there wasn't enough time to react.

He slipped into his sleeping back and laid on his back, listening to nature's orchestra. Whistling, dripping, whipping. They were all sounds he could handle.

He lay still for an hour, drifting in and out of sleep, until he heard the one sound he feared the most.

Footsteps.

CHAPTER 24

KARI KNUDSEN GRIPPED THE CONTROLS on the helicopter and tried to steady her hand. It wasn't a new sensation as it occurred every time she climbed into the cockpit. She used to love soaring over Svalbard's breathtaking landscape. But the pleasure of it all had left long ago; the act of operating a helicopter was little more than an exercise in self-flagellation.

After making her final checks, she turned on the engine, engaging the blades. Moments later, she was rising off the helipad at the Sysselmannen headquarters as Longyearbyen shrank beneath her.

Heading south toward Sorkapp Land, Knudsen had plenty of time to contemplate the mission as well as any other idea that came to mind. She preferred to dwell on the positive energy hovering around her life. As if being the most powerful person on an island wasn't enough for her, though that was never her ambition.

Knudsen dispensed with using society's metrics years ago. She refused to believe that how much money a person made in a year or how many awards someone won or how much power one possessed served as a true barometer of a person's success. She concluded that all of those elements and many others, whether tangible or abstract, led to the hyper-obsessive state that society had devolved into. No one was happy because everyone desired something they didn't—or couldn't—have. Such human machinations ceased to rule Knudsen long ago, or so she thought.

She felt just as hopeless and dissatisfied with life as everyone else she knew. Instead of longing for possessions or wealth or power or any other thing that only resulted in fleeting happiness, she longed for something else she couldn't have: She longed for her son back. For four years, she'd scraped out an existence in the doldrums, collecting scraps of happiness to try and replace the void created when Edvin died. And she wasn't succeeding.

She shuddered as she flew over the peak where it happened. Swallowing hard and struggling to choke back the tears, Knudsen flew on without glancing at the location a second time. People needed her help, and that's what she was going to do. Millions of people needed her help, especially the two men on the ground who dared to challenge the elements and an unknown criminal.

Perhaps he was known, maybe even to her, but it didn't make any difference. Her primary objective was to help the American secure the seeds. Helping Johansen save face at the Global Seed Vault was an added bonus. With all his contacts within the government, Johansen would be indebted to her for a long time. But Knudsen had no designs on holding it over Johansen's head; she intended to call in her favor the moment opportunity presented itself.

Knudsen swept across the valley, searching for any sign of the Russian thief. After having been on Svalbard for so long, she knew all the colors of every outfitters' snow suits as well as their routes. Visitors in the national parks were required to have an escort and were limited to a handful of passes each day. They also had to register with the Sysselmannen's office. Within a moment's glance, she could place each person, even as she hovered several hundred feet off the ground.

But so far, nothing out of the ordinary.

The task felt tedious if nothing else, proving to be little more than a cruel punishment where she was left with nothing to do but think and brood.

With the southern tip of Svalbard now visible, she was close to completing her sweep, and still nothing. If the Russian already escaped with the seeds, her opportunity to get what she truly wanted was gone with him. There'd be no trophy to return to Johansen so he could save face—or a big favor returned to her.

She decided to make one more pass near Hornsundtind peak when a flash of movement on the eastern side of the valley arrested her attention. She thought she saw a single sled team and a driver whose outfit she didn't recognize. Needing to take a closer look, she dropped lower and moved more slowly in her search.

Circling back around to the location where she first noticed the team, she methodically checked the area, just like she would on a search and rescue mission. The conditions were making it difficult to see—and difficult to fly.

She called back to headquarters to find out if there were any dogsled teams authorized to be in the national park. There weren't.

She smiled with a sense of satisfaction.

This is the man I'm looking for.

But her satisfaction quickly turned to angst as the helicopter lurched. Without hesitating, she left the area in search of a safe place to land.

No need in taking any chances in this weather.

Knudsen navigated to an area near the tip that was shielded by the wind. However, when she went outside and tried to walk back toward the location she'd seen the sled team, the weather beat her back.

She decided to wait out the storm and keep a watchful eye out for the mystery dogsled team.

CHAPTER 25

FLYNN AND LARSEN anchored in their dogs and set up a perimeter alarm. It would give them decent warning if a predator penetrated the boundary, but it didn't provide any level of protection. If a polar bear wanted to enter their camp, it'd have its way.

Despite the alarm, they agreed to take shifts watching the camp. Flynn appreciated the fact that this wasn't an activity performed in the dark, but it didn't mean he was any less tired or wouldn't struggle to stay awake. He was in desperate need of a good night's sleep, though he didn't know when he'd get one again.

Flynn volunteered to take the first shift, but not without receiving a litany of instructions from Larsen.

"If you know a bear has penetrated the perimeter, don't hesitate to shoot," Larsen said. "Before, we were in his territory, but if he comes into our camp, he's in our territory and he'll be looking for food, primarily us or the dogs."

"Roger that," Flynn said.

"Shoot center mass. Go for the kill. If you wound him, it's like any other combatant you face: It's only going to make him angrier and more determined to take you out."

Flynn nodded, not that he needed to be told these

things. He'd encountered bears in the wild before without any weapons and managed to survive, though he'd never engaged a polar bear. And he hoped he never would.

Flynn watched Larsen slip into the tent. Within ten minutes, he was snoring loudly.

That ought to keep every animal away from here.

Left with plenty of time to mull things over in his mind, Flynn chuckled to himself when he thought about how his original assignment of writing about the biopiracy fear and other conspiracies surrounding The Svalbard Global Seed Vault had morphed into an adventure race across the Arctic to save his country's corn seeds. He'd found himself thrust into unlikely predicaments in the past, but this one seemed to have implications that stretched far beyond the simple embarrassment of a conspiracy exposure. Hanging in the balance was the financial dominion of the world, at least that's what he'd been told. And while he was leery of any single entity wielding too much power, he trusted the American government with all its stop gaps and media freedom more than he did Russia. The results of a world market controlled by Russia frightened Flynn even more than a stalking polar bear.

After two hours, he switched with Larsen and fell asleep almost immediately.

Two hours later, Flynn awoke to a gentle nudge from Larsen.

"You're up," Larsen said.

Flynn staggered out of the tent and took his position at the lookout post. The wind continued to blast its way through the valley. However, Larsen's familiarity with the region led them to set up camp in the safety of a known enclave, limiting the effects of the weather.

Flynn sat almost motionless, nodding off several times before jerking upright and awake. But with about thirty minutes remaining in his shift, he heard something just outside their perimeter. Due to the way the rock face provided such good cover from the elements, it also hampered Flynn's ability to see much beyond a small opening. Only a sliver of the valley was viewable from his position.

He got up and walked toward the entrance in an effort to determine what the noise was.

"Hello?" Flynn called in a whisper, trying to keep his voice down so as not to waken Larsen. "Is anybody out there?"

Nothing.

Flynn waited for a few moments before turning around and walked back toward his post when he heard the same sound again. This time, he froze and craned his neck toward the opening, leaning with his ear.

"Hello?" Flynn whispered again.

Remaining still, he didn't return to his seat for two minutes.

Slowly sitting back down on his chair, Flynn wondered if he was just conjuring up sounds in his head. The sleep depravation and the self-imposed pressure of tracking down the Russian thief was starting to take a toll on his psyche. He was being tested in one of the most extreme environments coupled with an intense situation—and he felt like he was failing.

I've lost my edge. I don't know if I can do this any more.

Before Flynn had a chance to ponder just how dulled his skills had become, the perimeter alarm went off. Larsen squirmed out of the tent, stepping into his shoes and grabbing his gun.

Flynn stood up and dug his feet in, awaiting the predator.

Amidst Larsen fumbling around, Flynn couldn't discern between the scuffling of feet in the enclave and the footsteps outside of it. But it didn't matter much.

A polar bear rounded the corner and stormed right toward them. The dogs awakened from their slumber and began howling.

Larsen took the first shot, ripping a hole in the bear's upper arm but hardly slowing the beast down. The bear growled and staggered backward a few steps, crashing into the glacial wall behind him. Flynn fired next, hitting the bear in the chest. But it only seemed to make the bear angry.

Shocked by the tenacity of the animal, Flynn froze, wondering why the bear didn't drop to the ground. Larsen fired another shot at the bear's head, narrowly missing it. Snapped out of his momentary trance by Larsen's gunfire, Flynn began unloading on the animal, which had slowed considerably but had crawled toward the teams.

"The dogs!" Flynn cried before emptying his magazine on the bear.

By then, the bear was bleeding all over, its pristine white coat now stained crimson. Larsen fired a few more rounds at the bear, which had almost stopped moving forward. But in what seemed like a final gasp, he lunged at the dogs. The bear raked his claws across the two lead dogs on Flynn's team resulting in another bloody mess.

Larsen jammed another magazine into his gun and fired two more shots before the bear collapsed.

Flynn rushed over to the dogs.

"Flynn, don't!" warned Larsen.

Spinning around, Flynn's field of vision was almost filled

with a bloody paw swiping at his head.

Flynn leaned backward and turned his back to the incoming claw, avoiding a direct hit. The glancing blow did little more than rip his jacket and nick his arm. Without hesitating, he pulled the pistol out of his ankle holster and put two more close range shots in the bear's head.

The bear's arm crashed to the ground—and that time, it didn't move again.

"Are you all right?" Larsen asked.

Flynn inspected the damage. "It's just a scratch."

"What were you thinking?"

"I don't know. I—I was just worried about the dogs."

"This is the wild where survival is key. You about got yourself killed."

"But I didn't."

Larsen shook his head. "I know this is a new environment for you, operating up here in the Arctic and having to work with animals, but you can't let that compromise your good judgment."

Flynn nodded knowingly. His actions demonstrated that his instincts to protect extended beyond people.

"Come on," Larsen said. "Enough of a tongue lashing for tonight. Let's get these dogs fixed up."

Flynn stood up and looked at the behemoth animal lying lifeless at his feet, blood still pouring out of the holes they'd riddled his body with. It seemed like a waste of such a majestic animal.

Larsen stood next to Flynn and placed an arm around him.

"Don't feel too bad. Do you see how emaciated he was?"

Flynn nodded.

"He wasn't going to make it through the summer, maybe not even the end of the week. We were his last hope. It was either us or the dogs as food or death. We gave him a merciful ending. He won't suffer any more."

Larsen's words assuaged the twinge of guilt Flynn felt participating in a violent end to the bear. He'd killed dozens of men on missions before in the heat of battle, yet never once did he feel a sense of remorse. His enemy had purposefully chosen to impose his will on Flynn—and Flynn wasn't inclined to let it happen. His enemies' deaths were their own fault, men whose decisions put them at odds with American interests, men who didn't possess the skills and the wits to survive a confrontation with him.

A sharp tug on Flynn's pants leg snapped him out of his trance.

"Give me a hand with Champ, will you?" Larsen said. "He's got a nasty cut on his nose and we need to get it patched up."

"Do you think he can run?" Flynn asked.

Larsen gestured toward Champ's foot, which the dog held up limp.

"I doubt it. Looks like he took a nasty blow. But he's not the only one hurting."

Flynn looked at Charlie, the other dog that ran at the front with Champ. He, too, appeared to have an injury on his leg.

"What does this mean?"

"It means we're going to have to only run seven dogs tomorrow on each team and mix them up."

Flynn furrowed his brow. "Is that going to have much of an effect on our time?"

"Any time you remove your two strongest lead dogs, it's going to have a negative effect on the speed of the team," Larsen said. "It's also going to impact my team as well since we're going to have to create new teams and split up the two strongest lead dogs on my team."

"Can we catch the Russian thief like this?"

Larsen shrugged. "Depends on where he is, but we're certainly at a disadvantage now."

Flynn finished patching up Champ and Charlie and poked his head outside to check on the weather conditions in the valley. The sky was clear and the winds had almost died down completely.

The storm was gone.

CHAPTER 26

YOLKOV WHIRLED AROUND AND TRAINED his gun in the direction of the approaching footsteps. At any moment, he expected to see a pair of beady eyes and an enormous swath of white fur charging in his direction. He turned off the safety and eased his finger onto the trigger. But instead of seeing a bear, he saw a pair of boots and then another.

"No need to shoot," the man said, throwing his hands in the air.

"We're not here to eat you," said the other followed by a nervous laugh.

Yolkov dropped his weapon and studied the two familiar faces.

"I know you," Yolkov said. "You two were at the Barentsburg earlier this week and are filming a documentary."

They both nodded.

"Busted," the first man said. He extended his hand. "I'm Nigel Cameron."

"Collin Buckman," the other man said, also extending his hand.

Yolkov shook neither one of them, instead glaring at them in disgust.

"What do you two want?"

"World peace, a beautiful woman, fine wine, and England to win the World Cup," Nigel said.

"I'll settle for us to get out of bloody group play," Collin quipped.

"I'm not in the mood for visitors or any games," Yolkov said, raising his gun again.

Nigel threw his hands in the air.

"Yes, yes, of course. I'm sorry. My apologies," Nigel said. "I was just trying to make a joke. And I totally understand it's not funny to you, but I've grown tired of wasting my excellent wit on my camera man here."

"You have a camera?" Yolkov asked.

Collin nodded and patted his backpack. "Right here in my bag."

"Good," Yolkov said. "I want you to make a short video of me for my family in case I don't make it back out alive."

"Dear God, man, what are you going to do after you leave here?" Nigel asked.

"You're the one going to be leaving first if you know what's best for you. Come back down here next week, but it's not going to be safe over the next day."

Nigel stared at Yolkov. "And why's that?"

"You ask too many questions, the kind of questions that will get you killed." Yolkov turned toward Collin. "Can you make the video for me or not?"

Collin nodded. "Just give me a moment to set up my equipment."

He began to pull out his camera and tripod along with his microphone.

"Have you ever been on television before?" Nigel asked.

"Never intentionally."

"I see. Well, it's an interesting phenomenon when it comes to how people act in front of the camera. Even with nobody watching, they act like fools and—"

"Do you always talk this much?" Yolkov asked with a sneer.

"My apologies again, sir." Nigel took a deep breath. "May I ask what you're doing this far south on Svalbard by yourself?"

"My duty."

"To the mine?"

Yolkov pounded his heart with his fist.

"To Russia."

Visibly frustrated by Yolkov's evasive nature, Nigel knelt down to help Collin assemble all his gear.

Once they finished, Collin stood up and looked at Yolkov.

"Where would you like to film this?"

Yolkov found a location at the entrance of the cave.

"What about there? I want my son to see what a beautiful place this is."

"Looks like a wonderful spot," Collin said as he moved into position.

Collin handed Yolkov the lapel microphone, which he clipped onto his jacket.

"Ready?" Collin asked.

Yolkov nodded.

"Start speaking whenever you like," Collin said.

Yolkov cleared his throat and adjusted his stance and posture, sliding his feet closer together and straightening his back. He clasped his hands together in front of himself and began.

"Alex and Boris, I come to you today from the beautiful scenery in Svalbard, and I'm making this message because I fear I may never see you again if I'm unsuccessful. I'm on a mission for the Russian government, and if I fail, my punishment may be harsh, either through death or lifetime imprisonment by some other unjust government. Just know that I did this for you. I had no choice in the matter, but I believed that if I succeeded, I would be able to make a better life for all of us.

"Living in Barentsburg for the past three years has given me sufficient time to reflect on our lives and the future. And I've decided I want it to be better than what it was. I want us to be free to enjoy one another's company without fear of where or even if we will get our next meal. Life is too short to worry about such things, so I am doing something that will remove that fear from our lives and let us be a family again, one that lives together, plays together, and laughs together.

"However, if I fail, just know that's what I died chasing—a dream for us to have a better way of life. I don't desire possessions as much as I desire time with you both. I look forward to seeing you both very soon."

Yolkov blew a kiss toward the camera and then stated his address in Perm so Collin could send a copy of it to Alexis and Boris. Yolkov then motioned for Collin to end the recording.

Nigel shook his head as he looked at Yolkov, their eyes locked.

"What exactly are you going to do?" Nigel asked as he broke his gaze to glance at the sled and the seeds sitting on it.

"I think it's time you leave," Yolkov said.

Nigel moved slowly toward the cave entrance while

Collin hurriedly stuffed the equipment back into his bag.

"Leave now," Yolkov shouted, unsatisfied with Nigel's slow pace.

Yolkov stood at the entrance to watch the two men stumble along for a few paces before Nigel pulled out his phone and started dialing a number. Pulling out his gun, Yolkov fired a shot in the air, freezing Nigel and Collin.

"End that call and throw me your phone—or the next shot goes through your chest," Yolkov said.

Nigel put his hands up, holding the cell phone high in the air. He tossed it toward Yolkov.

"You, too," Yolkov said, pointing at Collin.

Collin dug into his pocket and tossed his phone toward Yolkov as well.

"Good luck and thank you," Yolkov said as he waved them off with the back of his hand.

He didn't move for the next ten minutes as he watched them trudge northward. While they were overly inquisitive, Yolkov was confident they wouldn't be able to report his location to the Sysselmannen before the morning when he met Berezin at the water's edge. Yolkov was done killing, even if his mission required it. That ruthless instinct he lived with for so long, the one that reflexively emerged when he was confronted with taking the dogs from the Longyearbyen Kennel, felt painful to re-engage with. He was determined to bury that part of his past, so much so, that there he was, going against his better judgment, the same judgment that cost him his place in the Spetsnaz.

Fifteen minutes later, he wondered if he'd come to regret his goodwill toward them.

***

YOLKOV'S ALARM ON HIS WATCH beeped and he awoke quickly. At 5:00 a.m. on Tuesday morning, he had thirty minutes to assemble the team and get going if he hoped to arrive at the drop point at 7:00 a.m. He dished out food for the dogs and quickly repacked. Once he finished packing, he looked outside to check the weather. It was near-perfect conditions, standing in stark contrast to the seemingly endless parade of storms that pounded Svalbard for the previous few days.

Scanning the area before embarking on the short thirty-kilometer journey ahead, Yolkov seemed satisfied that they could travel the necessary distance without getting caught by anyone.

As long as the Sysselmannen doesn't fly over in her helicopter.

If the Sysselmannen had indeed returned to Longyearbyen, he doubted she would make the long journey down the southern point after turning back the day before.

For the next hour and a half, Yolkov mushed ahead. With each passing minute, his anticipation grew stronger. He looked forward to seeing his family. He looked forward to the reward. He looked forward to a new life. In the days since he first started, he'd come to realize that he didn't want his old job with the Spetsnaz back. It was the end of the line; one final mission for the motherland.

With reality settling in for Yolkov, a man whose identity had been immersed in his role with the Spetsnaz, he couldn't help but reflect how his time serving with the Russian special forces had changed him. Carrying out atrocities in the name of direct orders expedited the removal of all such compassion from his life. He killed defenseless farmers because they proved to be stubborn roadblocks to achieving Spetsnaz missions. He hung thieves in the forest and planted explosives in separatists' camps. The taking of another person's life had become rote. Yet a full extraction hadn't occurred. A modicum of compassion remained, one that ultimately led to his dismissal. He'd never forget it—or regret it, no matter how disappointing the outcome.

Yolkov had been assigned to secure a small building in a remote location of the Black Forest for the Russian trade minister. Highly regarded and respected as a family man, the trade minister was anything but that, as Yolkov quickly learned. On that particular detail, he discovered that the location was used as a place to conceal the trade minister's extracurricular sexual exploits.

That evening while the trade minister was finishing his final engagement, Yolkov found a Chinese woman lurking in the bushes. She was dressed up and appeared as though she might have been a guest who escaped from the party. He radioed to the guard at the entrance to find out if she was on any guest lists. She wasn't. Despite the appearances, he knew the truth: none of those women were there on their own accord. Many of them were married and taken there against their will, forced to commit a litany of unmentionable acts.

Yolkov was under strict orders to shoot on sight anyone perceived to be a threat—and she fit the profile. Foreign, beautiful, muscular, and lurking around in the forest. She held her hands up in surrender as Yolkov approached her.

"What are you doing here?" Yolkov asked.

"I came back for revenge. Do you know what that man in there did to me?"

Yolkov swallowed hard and shook his head.

"I'm not particularly interested either. What's done is done."

"But it doesn't have to keep being done."

Yolkov agreed, but he couldn't voice his affirmation, at least not audibly. He never knew who might be listening to their conversation.

"There are other avenues to express your grievances."

"Avenues that aren't dead ends, always built to ensure a guaranteed outcome for some elitist politician? That's definitely an avenue I'd like to explore . . . right after I kill him."

"Look, just be patient. I don't want to have to hurt you, but you're not making it easy right now for me to restrain myself."

"Why? Because my loyalty isn't blind?"

"No, it's just that—"

Another guard, gun drawn, hustled toward him. "What's this?" the guard demanded. "We were under strict orders to shoot any intruders on sight."

"I'm not an intruder," the woman said. "I've been invited."

The guard furrowed his brow. "They why are you—"

With the stealth of an assassin, the woman darted behind the guard and snapped his neck. She then turned and looked at Yolkov.

"Take his gun and get your revenge," Yolkov said.

Ten minutes later, she murdered the trade minister, shooting him directly between the eyes. In the initial investigation, a soldier standing nearby claimed that he saw Yolkov release the woman, even letting her walk away with the guard's gun. Without hesitating, Yolkov concocted a story about how she incapacitated him by putting him to sleep first before obviously dealing with the other guard later. An admission of guilt was as good as suicide. When Yolkov contested the other witnesses' events, he left the military tribunal unsure who to believe. A split decision meant there would be no corporal punishment or prison sentence for him, but it did result in an emotional flogging as a general stripped Yolkov's ranking and discharged him from service.

Years later, Yolkov still didn't regret what he did. The trade minister acted abhorrently, preying on women and using his power to gratify his uncontrollable lust. Not that he was any different than most of the top level brass when it came to abusing his position. Yolkov took solace in the fact that he still had a faint semblance of a pulse when it came to kindness. There were two filmmakers still alive who could attest to that.

Once he was about five kilometers away, he used his satellite phone to contact Berezin aboard the Russian sub.

"I'm approaching the drop location," Yolkov said. "How far away are you?"

"We just launched a dinghy. I'll be there with two other men in about ten minutes. Do you still have the package?"

"Yes, sir. It's all here and accounted for."

"Excellent work, comrade."

Yolkov continued mushing ahead when a gunshot cracked through the valley, causing him to bring his team to a halt. He crouched behind the sled and tried to scan the area. He tossed the anchor into the ground and carefully rammed it into the ice with his heel. The dogs broke into a mournful chorus interspersed with vicious growls and sad whimpers. As he was searching for the location of the shooter, another bullet whistled near him, hitting the ground a few feet away. Snow splattered onto the sled and Yolkov. He studied the marking and tried to figure out the trajectory of the bullet and quickly deduced the shots were coming from a shooter behind a rock about 150 meters away. He slowly reached for his gun before another shot, closer than the last one, landed just inches from the sled.

Yolkov knew when he'd been beaten and raised his hands in surrender.

CHAPTER 27

KNUDSEN STUDIED THE MAN'S MOVEMENTS through her scope as she stepped from behind a boulder. Any slight motion and she'd drop him right where he stood. And though she couldn't be certain, she trusted he realized that.

Her suspicion was confirmed when he stepped slowly off the sled and raised his hands in the air. Cautiously and methodically, she walked down the slow rise toward the man, who stood just to the side of his sled and was no more than twenty meters from the frothy sea lashing against the land. That short distance to the water was a muddy mess, devoid of any snow to speak of due to the warmer coastal weather.

With the gun trained on him, she steadily eased her way nearer until she slowed her gait at ten meters.

"You speak English?" she asked.

The man nodded.

"I know you," she said. "Don't you work at Barentsburg?"

He nodded again.

"You're going to need to come with me."

The man feigned innocence. "What did I do? You can't detain me without telling me why? This is not Russia."

She smiled and shook her head. "No, it's not. But I think you know what you did."

Knudsen gestured toward the bags of seed on the sled. "Breaking and entering the seed vault, stealing seeds. We've got more than enough to deport you to the mainland and convict you for a long prison sentence."

The man bent down and picked up a bag of the seeds. "These seeds? You think I stole this?"

"Whatever it is you're trying to do, it isn't going to work. We both know you're not riding around on a dog sled with corn seeds for the fun of it. Now, drop the bag and step away from the sled."

The Russian stared her down, eyeing her closely.

"I don't think I'm going to do any such thing."

Knudsen bristled at his defiance. "You do understand that I'm the one holding the gun, don't you?" She clicked the safety off and eased her finger onto the trigger.

"I also understand that this bag right here is so precious to the United States that people would pay me millions for it. I think we both know what's at stake here."

She glared at him. "If you don't do as I ask, I won't hesitate to shoot you."

Knudsen was so focused on the Russian that she didn't even hear the footsteps approaching behind her.

"You've already hesitated to shoot him," a man said.

Knudsen glanced over her shoulder to see a Russian military commander striding ashore toward her flanked by a pair of guards, all of whom had their guns drawn.

CHAPTER 28

FLYNN URGED HIS TEAM FORWARD as it struggled after losing its two leaders to injuries. To help distribute the weight more evenly, Larsen put Charlie on his sled, while Champ rested comfortably on Flynn's sled. However, the seven-dog team didn't run as fast or tight as before. Yet there was no recourse for Flynn and Larsen other than to mush along.

As they came around a bend, the southern tip of Sorkapp Land came into view. And when it did, Flynn almost lost his breath.

"Do you see that?" Flynn said, pointing ahead.

In the distance, Flynn made out five people standing near a dog sled. As they got closer, it appeared to be some sort of a standoff, as they almost all appeared to have weapons drawn.

"We're going to lose our chance if these dogs don't run faster," Flynn said.

"They're going as fast as they can," Larsen said. "They don't run that fast when it's this warm or when the snow has turned to slush. Plus, we're both running with incomplete teams and combinations that aren't exactly going to result in top speeds."

"So, you're saying we're screwed?"

Larsen kept his gaze straight ahead.

"Just keep mushing. Maybe they'll stick around long enough for us to get there in time."

Flynn estimated they were about a kilometer and a half away, though that would still take about five minutes based on their current pace. Flynn said a quick prayer under his breath and pleaded with the dogs to run faster.

"What's your plan when we get there?" Larsen asked.

"I intend on grabbing the corn seed by force, if I have to," Flynn said.

"It won't be that easy. We're outnumbered for one."

Flynn shrugged. "Do you think you can take out one of the guards?"

"Yeah. That shouldn't be a problem."

"I can take out the other two soldiers."

"And the thief?"

"I'm going to have to take a flyer and hope the Sysselmannen shoots him."

Larsen shook his head. "I don't watch many American westerns, but I saw a John Wayne movie once. And this feels a lot like that, except we're not riding on horses."

"Well, the Duke hardly ever died."

"This isn't Hollywood."

Flynn shook his head. "And I don't shoot like a cowboy. I won't be trying to shoot a gun out of anyone's hand up there. Kill shots only."

"I hope you're right about this."

"I hope we live to debate it."

As they approached within a hundred meters, Flynn watched in horror as the scenario took a drastic turn for the worse. The commander grabbed the Sysselmannen and jammed a gun to her head. They began to ease their way backward toward the dinghy waiting on the shoreline to take them back to their submarine located about a hundred meters off shore.

Flynn and Larsen both pulled out their guns just before coming to a stop at the edge of the snow line.

"That's far enough," yelled the commander, who stepped gingerly on the rocks scattered across a small area of land uncovered by snow.

Flynn looked at the two guards, both toting a bag of corn seed while keeping their guns trained on him and Larsen.

"Where do you think you're going with that, comrade?" Flynn shouted.

"Settle down," the commander said. "We don't want an international incident here."

"It's a little late for that."

The commander tightened his grip on the Sysselmannen, whose futile squirms produced nothing but more pain.

"I don't think you want her blood on your hands, do you, Mr. Flynn?" the commander said.

Flynn was stunned that the commander knew his name but tried not to show it, remaining stoic and quiet.

"That's right. I know who you are. I'd receive a hero's welcome if I came back with your dead body. However, that's not the mission, just like yours isn't to assassinate a high-ranking commander in the Russian Army. Either way, you lose. Even if you get your seeds, you're going to have to kill me to do it—and I can assure you that will lead to a war."

Flynn narrowed his eyes. "Bring her back along with the seeds right now."

The commander laughed mockingly. "Bring her back? And the seeds? Or what? What exactly are you going to do, Mr. Flynn?"

Flummoxed, Flynn had no response. He knew when he'd been beaten. He was outmanned and outgunned. There was no way he was going to get the seeds and the Sysselmannen back alive without a stroke of luck. And there wasn't one to be found.

The commander moved quietly back toward the water's edge.

"That's right. Good boy," the commander said. "You live to fight another day. Of course, we might not be in this predicament if the Sysselmannen weren't so kind-hearted. She spared my comrade's life even though his actions will result in thousands upon thousands of people starving as you Americans will close ranks and forget about the rest of the world. You'll pay fifty dollars for a pound of beef if there are any cattle deemed worthy enough to save. And you'll let the world burn. And we'll expose you and your corrupt politicians for who they really are."

"You have a twisted view of America," Flynn shot back.

"No, I don't, comrade. But you lack the fortitude to do what needs to be done in times of conflict, just like your Sysselmannen here. All she had to do was—"

The commander pulled the trigger on his gun as the shot echoed through the valley. However, it wasn't directed at Knudsen. Instead, it was aimed at the Russian operative who stole the seeds.

The man crumpled to the ground, gasping for air as blood spewed from the wound in his head.

"Thank you for your devotion, comrade Yolkov," the

commander said as he returned the barrel of the gun to Knudsen's head. "You served your country well and she thanks you."

After a few moments of awkward silence while Yolkov bled out, Flynn ran the scenarios in his head to see if that gave him an opportunity to strike. Any fleeting ideas were dashed the moment several armed naval officers climbed atop the submarine and stood at attention. One shot and the place would devolve into a powder keg. Flynn figured he might be able to kill the commander, but Knudsen and the seeds would be lost. And then there was Larsen to think about.

Flynn looked at Larsen and slightly shook his head. Concluding that this wasn't the time to be itching for a fight, Flynn stood frozen as he watched Knudsen and the target assets motor back toward the submarine.

"Goodbye, Mr. Flynn," the commander said. "Tell your friends in Washington that Commander Berezin has outwitted them again. They'll know what that means."

Knudsen looked over her shoulder at him, worry lines chiseled into her forehead. Help me, she mouthed. The commander noticed what she was doing and grabbed her face with his hand before slapping her.

Flynn took a deep breath and tried to stay clam. A fantasy flashed through his mind where he riddled Berezin with bullets. But now wasn't the time. He had to wait.

The commander smiled and waved mockingly with his free hand.

Go ahead and laugh, commander. You haven't seen the last of me.

CHAPTER 28

Omsk, Russia

GROMOV GLARED AT HIS SON as he paced around the office. He breathed heavily, trying to gain control of his emotions before he threw objects around the room and destroyed it, or worse. Vladimir was the root source of his anger and Gromov pondered that maybe a paperweight to the head would help his son regain some level of sensibility.

Gromov finally felt composed enough to speak. He stopped pacing and leaned forward on his knuckles across the conference room table toward Vladimir, who sat still, lips tightly clamped shut.

"What did I tell you about our expansion plans? I believe I told you to wait," Gromov said, answering his own question. "I'm quite certain you didn't hear me or else you wouldn't have done such an idiotic thing, now would you?"

Vladimir shook his head.

"But you did hear me, didn't you?"

Vladimir remained silent.

Gromov slapped the table top. "I said, didn't you?"

Vladimir nodded slowly, refusing to utter a word.

"Do you realize what you just did?" Gromov started to

pace again as he felt the blood rush to his face. "Do you realize that you could have bankrupted this country? What if
things don't go the way we want them to? What if the price
of wheat suddenly crashes? Then what? We can't have all
our cash resources tied up in wheat if we're unable to ascer-
tain the direction of the markets."

Vladimir furrowed his brow.

"How can we ever determine the future direction of
anything in the market?"

Gromov stopped and smiled.

"Now that's the first intelligent question you've asked
me since you started working for me. Do you think I created
Gromov Global off of good fortune and unexplainable
market shifts?" He laughed. "No, no, no. I built Gromov
Global off the knowledge that all of the things that are
happening in the market right now were going to happen."

"But how?"

Gromov held up his index finger and walked around
briefly before answering.

"I can't tell you everything, son. But what I can tell you
is that you must learn to trust me and listen to me. When I
say, wait, you wait. In due time I will tell you more, but for
now this is what I want to stress to you."

Vladimir nodded, hanging his head, staring down at the table.

"Head up, son. I could torture you in unimaginable ways,
but I'll only make you tell Mother why our deal to buy her
dream home in Madeira just fell through. Since it's your fault,
it seems like a reasonable punishment."

"Come on, Father. Don't make me tell her."

"Better you than me. Now, run home and go deliver the
news."

Vladimir got up and walked toward the door when Gromov's phone rang.

"Gromov," he said as he answered.

"Comrade Gromov, I was asked to call you at the behest of Commander Berezin."

"Go on. I've been expecting your call."

"He wanted me to pass along the message to you than the seeds were secured this morning and are in Russian possession."

A smile spread across Gromov's face.

"And where exactly are these seeds?"

"They are on a Russian sub headed for port. I will give you more details as they become available."

Vladimir stopped at the door and turned the knob.

"You sure are happy all of a sudden," he said, grousing.

"As you should be too," Gromov said.

"Why's that?"

"Everything I was waiting on just came together. I now stand fully behind your decision to initiate the expansion as soon as possible."

"Wait, what?" Vladimir said as he released the door handle and sat back down. "Explain to me what just happened here because I don't understand?"

"In order to move forward, I needed assurances that the market would hold steady for a while. Now I know it will."

Vladimir shook his head. "How can anyone get guarantees about the market?"

"I can and I just did. Don't worry about the how—just acquaint yourself with the what."

"I'm not sure I understand."

"The question you need to be asking now is, 'What now,

Father?'" Gromov said. "You're going to be a very busy young man in the days ahead."

"So, you're not upset anymore that the sale of Mother's dream home just fell through on my account?"

Gromov walked next to his son and put his arm around him.

"Oh, no, Son. I'm not upset at all. I may not have the cash on hand right now to buy Mother a dream home, but very soon I'll have enough cash to buy her a dream island. We're going to be rich beyond your wildest expectations."

CHAPTER 30

Washington, D.C.

SENATOR POWELL WENT FOR A SWIM at his athletic club and tried to steer clear of the televisions blaring in every room. None of them painted the kind of picture necessary to quell the market fears; rather, they did nothing but stoke the fears of an already terrified nation. One report chronicled several families in various locations across the country who had adopted the bunker mentality. The report went on to prove that these stories weren't merely anecdotal when analyzing the empirical data. Canned goods sales spiked, gun and ammunition sales reached all-time highs, more than a dozen survival skill books rocketed into the top 20 on The New York Times non-fiction bestseller list. Then there were the sad reports of farmers talking about how they were going to lose land that had been in their family for six generations.

Powell shoved earplugs into his ears to prepare for his swim and contemplated leaving them in all day. Nobody had anything to say that he wanted to hear. Whether it was on the television or in person, he'd descended into a swirling nightmare of apocalyptic proportions. For forty-five minutes, he hoped to escape the cesspool of blame, anger, and outright lies of people who seemed intent on drowning him in it before he ever had an opportunity to turn things around.

The steady rhythm of his long strokes that fought against the water seemed like a perfect picture of what he faced in the days ahead.

Just keep swimming.

The problem for Powell was that he couldn't see the shore or even know if one existed. Learning the fate of the seeds at the vault in Svalbard would at least provide him with the direction necessary to navigate through the growing political mess. Without it, he'd simply be treading water. And that wouldn't be good enough for the President. And it'd certainly harm Powell's chances at winning the Secretary of State post.

At least the President's offer provided Powell with some more political capital. And while he was swimming, he decided he wouldn't waste time trying to decide when to spend it. With the way the nation was crumbling, he figured there'd be no use in saving it for the future.

After he showered and got dressed, Powell got into his car and called Fenestra CEO Phillip Wilson again.

"I'm sorry, Senator, but Mr. Wilson is extremely busy today," Wilson's secretary said after Powell demanded to speak with him.

"This can't wait."

"I'm afraid it's going to have to. He's in meetings all day and won't be available until the end of the week."

Powell took a deep breath and exhaled slowly in an attempt to calm down.

"Look, Cindy, or whatever the hell your name is, I need to talk with Mr. Wilson right now."

"I'm going to hang up now, sir."

Click.

Powell growled and thought for a minute before calling his assistant.

"Can you get me the cell number for Phillip Wilson, CEO of Fenestra?"

"Certainly, Mr. Powell."

She returned to the phone shortly with the number.

"Thank you."

He hung up and blocked his number before he dialed Wilson.

"Phillip Wilson," he said as he answered.

Powell was about to speak but waited for a moment, listening to the background sounds. A seagull screeching, a buoy clanging, the low roar of a ship's horn as it approached the harbor. He didn't need a GPS tracker to know where Wilson was.

"Mr. Wilson, this is Senator Powell."

Powell heard an exasperated breath forced out by Wilson.

"Senator, I thought we already went over everything that you asked for—and I said no?"

Powell knew that Wilson docked a large yacht in Miami. He knew because he'd been to parties on that very boat on numerous occasions as the guest of Mr. Wilson. Such knowledge came in handy when manipulating a conversation. In fact, Powell had so done his homework on Wilson that the Senator anticipated the CEO's response three to four exchanges in advance.

"With the stock market tanking and a world food crisis looming—one which your company helped create—I find it interesting that you're chumming it up with your buddies on your yacht right now. I wonder how fast the media could get down to your boat?"

"Don't try to play games with me, Senator. You've spent more than your fair share of hours on this very boat."

Powell smiled, satisfied with the direction of the conversation.

"Look, I'm not here to fight. In fact, I think we need to rally together and stand with one another in a time such as this."

"Don't you mean, do your bidding?" Wilson scoffed. "Sorry, but I'm not interested."

"No, no. That's not what I'm suggesting at all. What I'm trying to say is that there are dark days ahead; there are also opportunities. And more than ever, we need each other. Whether it's today or ten years from now, cooperation is the key to achieving greatness in our line of work."

"And if I was interested, what exactly do you have to offer, Senator?"

Even though Powell tried to script out the conversation in advance, he was still pleasantly surprised that Wilson had remained engaged and not completely written him off.

"There's some turbulence ahead in Washington; turbulence for one person, career launch for another."

"Get to the point."

"The President asked me if I could help him calm the fears of the American people," Powell began. "There's too much uncertainty as it pertains to the world markets. Russia appears to have orchestrated a brazen food grab while simultaneously funding eco-terrorism. It puts us in a precarious situation, our entire nation, really. If the world believes

Russia possesses the lion's share of global crops, including wheat, we won't be able to stop the accelerated growth of the futures market. In a few months time, we'll plunge into a depression, one in which people can't even afford food with the money they still have. And I think it's in both our best interests that this doesn't happen."

"And you'd just wave your magic wand and do this as a favor to the President?"

Powell clucked his tongue. "Now, now, Mr. Wilson. No need for such cynicism. However, I wouldn't just do it out of the goodness of my own heart. Everyone in Washington ultimately has their own political interests to look after. But the president did offer me a prominent position that wields quite a bit of power both in the U.S. and abroad."

"Is this the kind of position Don Kramer might be resigning from soon?"

"It just might be," Powell said, trying to give every indication with his excited inflection that it was exactly that kind of position.

Wilson grunted. "Well, I could always use a close ally in the State Department. And who better of an ally than the Secretary of State himself?"

"I'd say none, Mr. Wilson."

"Okay, you've made your point, Senator. We'll put out a press release before noon."

"Excellent. See, Mr. Wilson, I told you that we'd do better working together than trying to tear each other apart."

"Even a broken clock ..." Wilson mumbled before hanging up.

You can insult me all you want—just as long as you do what I ask.

At noon, Powell watched the news in his office while he ate his lunch. He preferred to do business with two-hour power lunches, but based on the current political climate, he decided it might be more soothing to eat alone. However, the cable news reports did little to ease his anxiety. That is until Sunny Poole, the anchor whose name belied her seriousness as a newscaster, delivered a breaking news update.

Fenestra just announced that they will commit to having a full allotment of non-GMO corn seeds in time for next season. This early report has already reached the markets, and corn futures are dropping, as are wheat futures. Financial analysts are already calling this announcement the kind of bold leadership we need in times of crisis. However, there are still some skeptics who want to know just where Fenestra houses these facilities since last week it was reported that LES sabotaged every such facility in the U.S., leaving prospects bleak next season for corn growers. Surprisingly, Fenestra also promised to maintain prices from this season amid fears of price gouging for a limited supply of its products.

Powell didn't appreciate her editorialization of the news. Catch phrases and words like "some skeptics" and "surprisingly" was how Sunny Poole developed a committed band of followers on social media. Her snarky quips were often turned into Vine loops or posted to YouTube and shared millions of times, often without comment. And people seemed to trust her, even when her biased treatment of a story was as obvious as the other two reasons she had quickly developed into one of the popular television broadcasters.

But for once, Powell didn't fret over Sunny's barbs. The effects were already taking place. She could ask her tough questions, but the people had already heard that Fenestra, the biggest seed manufacturer in the world, wasn't going to let America's corn crop fail.

Step One to quell the public's fears? Check.

The next part of Powell's assignment meant actually having something for seed manufacturers to work with. He didn't care if Fenestra was the one handling them or not. All that mattered was that U.S. farmers were able to produce a third of the world's corn again. But nothing would happen without the seeds. And that entire mission rested on the shoulders of James Flynn.

Powell called Flynn and hoped he not only answered but also had good news.

"Senator Powell," Flynn said, "I hope you're day is going better than mine."

"How well my day is going is directly connected to yours."

Flynn sighed. "I wish I had better news for you, but at this point, I don't."

"What happened?"

"Turns out some Russian special forces operative managed to get the seeds from the vault to a Russian sub stationed off shore before we had a chance to intercept them," Flynn said. "They kidnapped the Sysselmannen, too. I didn't think they really needed her as an insurance policy since the seeds are so valuable, but the commander panicked and thought he needed her to escape back to the sub."

"So, what's anybody doing about it?"

"Nothing yet. You're the first person I've told about this. I'm working with a guide here to get these dogs onto a helicopter and fly them back to Longyearbyen."

"And then what?"

"If you think I can be of any service to you, I will go after them. I've conducted ops in Russia before and am familiar with their protocols. If we wait very long, we might lose them and the seeds will be gone for good."

"Tell me what you need and I'll makes a few calls to the Department of Defense and see what I can do."

"I'll need transportation to get me near the port of call that seems the most likely destination."

"We always have subs in that area, so that shouldn't be a problem."

"I'll call you after I've landed in Longyearbyen and let you know what else I need."

"Any chance you think you can get your hands on these seeds by Friday?"

"Why Friday?"

"Never mind. Just do your best and serve your country well."

It wasn't a perfect start to the first half of his Tuesday, but Powell wasn't complaining after how the previous few days had gone.

***

THREE HOURS LATER, one of the Sysselmannen's deputies landed the helicopter near the southern most tip of Svalbard in Sorkapp Land and Flynn exited the aircraft. Larsen stayed right behind him.

"Where do you think you're going?" Flynn asked.

"With you, of course," Larsen said. "You're going to need help getting the Sysselmannen back."

Flynn's face dropped. "Did you think I was going after her? I'm sorry if I gave you that impression. I've only been tasked with recovering the seeds. The issue with Knudsen is a diplomatic one between Norway and Russia."

"You're just going to leave her? You can't do that. They'll kill her."

"Sometimes you have to pick your battles."

"This time, the battle has picked you—and it includes extracting two things from the Russians: the seeds and Kari Knudsen."

"Do you understand the logistical nightmare this will create? It's challenging enough to sneak out of Russia by yourself if you're on your own. The last time I was here, I needed help to get myself out. I can't imagine how daunting it would be to try and escape with her."

"Don't imagine. Find out from personal experience by trying. You know you've got to. You can't let her rot in a Russian prison somewhere for simply being in the wrong place at the wrong time. You're better than that."

Flynn sighed and nodded. "I know you're right. I just don't see how it can be done."

"Figure out a way then."

Flynn shook Larsen's hand. "I'll do my best, though my past work in intelligence tells me that she probably isn't even alive. If she is, I promise not to leave her behind. And one day when I come back here, we'll finish that beer we were having before all this started."

After a few minutes, a dinghy appeared.

"Looks like my ride is here," Flynn said, looking at the water.

A small motor-powered dinghy cut through the sea's rough waters, heading straight toward them. Instead of an American sub, Senator Powell's vast network of politicians and owed favors resulted in a Finnish fishing boat.

"What is that?" Larsen asked as he looked at the Vahvuus.

Flynn took a deep breath and shook his head.

"So much for getting a pleasant night of sleep."

Larsen smiled and nodded before he reached around Flynn's back and pulled out his satellite phone from his backpack and dropped it in the snow.

Flynn never felt anything.

CHAPTER 31

Barents Sea
Aboard the K-329 Severodinsk

KNUDSEN TRIED TO LIE DOWN on the small cot that jutted out from the wall in the brig. She was used to being on boats that pitched and rolled across the water, not a boat that cut right through it. Even so, it still wasn't the smooth ride she imagined a submarine to be, and her stomach was also in sharp disagreement with her current sleeping arrangement.

She banged on the door and yelled for anyone who could hear here.

"Can I get a glass of water, please?" she said. "I'm very thirsty and my stomach doesn't feel well."

She waited a few seconds and didn't hear a reply or even footfalls on the sub's steel floor.

"I can promise you that it will not be pleasant to clean up."

A minute later, a guard handed her a plastic cup of water through the bars in the door.

"Spasibo," she said as she took the cup.

The guard grunted and plodded down the hallway, his footsteps echoing against the ship's steel encasement.

After she finished drinking the water, Knudsen tried out the cot again, this time twisting and turning, unable to catch even a few minutes of sleep. She struggled to doze off for half an hour before Commander Berezin made his way down to the brig.

"Welcome to the Severodinsk, Ms. Knudsen. How is your stay?"

Face forward, eyes locked onto a certain spot on the wall, she ignored him as she sat on the edge of the cot.

Berezin ran his fingers along the brig's prison door bars. At first, it was fast. Then he slowed it down to a deliberate pace.

Thump . . . thump . . . thump.

This exercise lasted for the better part of five minutes, yet Knudsen remained stoic until the last one was made.

"Suit yourself," Berezin said. "If you don't want to talk, you could've at least alerted me so I didn't waste both our times."

Knudsen finally spoke, standing up and walking toward the door before she uttered a word.

"Do you have a pillow? It's difficult to sleep on that thing without wrenching my back."

Berezin's eyes danced as he engaged in a mind game with Knudsen.

"Of course you can, dear. Let me have one of the crewmen bring one down."

Berezin disappeared and could be heard mumbling something down the hall. A few minutes later, he returned with a pillow in his hand.

Knudsen reached through the bars and tried to grab the pillow.

"Nuh-uh-uh-uhh," he said. "I need you to do something for me first before you can have this."

She stared him down, refusing to show the true anger raging within her.

"What is it?" she asked.

He smiled. "I have a few special favors I'd like for you to commit with me in my quarters."

She didn't need him to spell out his intentions.

He fumbled with the keys on his key ring, searching for the right one. Once he identified it, he shoved it into the lock and began to turn it.

Berezin reached for her hand and took it. She withdrew it from him.

"I never agreed to do anything with you," she snapped.

He ignored her, waving her off with his hand.

"There are two ways we can go about this: A luxurious moment or two in my bed or a forceful demonstration of how to take something that's rightfully yours."

She spun and spit in his face, following it up with an attempted slap. Before she could make contact with his face, Berezin grabbed her wrist and prevented it from going any farther.

"You're a pig, you know that?"

He broke into a hearty laugh and re-secured the door.

"Perhaps later then, when you're in the mood."

Knudsen slumped against the wall and broke into tears. She knew that there were people like him in the world, but she'd never encountered one so ruthless. Enduring offhanded comments about her gender as a top official within the Norwegian law enforcement system was bearable, if not expected. But the Russian commander intended to commit heinous acts against her simply because he could.

She'd never felt more helpless in her life.

Her anger gave way to despair, which led to heaving sobs. Eventually even her cramped quarters couldn't prevent exhaustion as she drifted off to sleep.

Within what seemed like mere minutes after dozing off, Knudsen sat straight up and opened her eyes wide, concerned about alarms blaring throughout the ship. Between the intermittent blasts of warning signals, Knudsen heard the heavy footfalls of soldiers rushing to their posts. Team leaders barked out orders. The chaos swirling just beyond her door seemed urgent, if not dire.

"What's happening?" she called.

Not a single soldier made time to explain.

"Someone tell me what's going on?"

A bell sounded before the sub pointed its nose downward and dove farther into the depths of the Barents Sea.

The chatter among the crew members reached Knudsen's ears but sounded more like nervous instructions than serious commands. Without an explanation, she ran through the list of possible scenarios in her head.

Were they performing evasive maneuvers because they were being pursued by another sub? Were they about to launch a nuclear weapon? Was there a global armageddon already taking place?

She didn't have the imagination for anything. The possibilities all seemed dire, and all with hopeless outcomes.

After a half hour of those intense exercises with the sub shaking and rattling, it stopped. The crew she could hear from her cell seemed to collectively exhale a sigh of relief.

When one of the sailors ventured near the brig, she

begged him to tell her what had happened.

"Nothing for you to worry about," he said.

"Where are we going? Can you tell me that?"

"In a few more hours, we will be docking in the Severo-morsk Harbor."

"But wait," Knudsen said.

The soldier kept walking without glancing back at her.

Knudsen's despair slowly morphed into rage over the rest of their voyage. She'd been captured simply to help the soldiers escape with their lives in the standoff at the shore. The fact that she was still alive meant that she was an insurance policy until they reached port. Once they had no more use for her, they'd kill her—that much she was sure of.

She needed to come up with a way to make herself more valuable until she could figure out a way to escape.

The idea wasn't novel, but it was her best hope at survival.

She put her anger aside and started to think.

CHAPTER 32

Southern coast of Svalbard

FLYNN THOUGHT LARSEN'S REQUEST to join him on the dinghy was rather odd, though the captain of the Vahvuus denied it based on time constraints. Larsen was relegated to waving from the shore. Whoever had made the official request to have the ship pick up Flynn incentivized the captain for expediency, according to one of the crew members on the dinghy. With such favors being tossed around and desperate measures being discussed, Flynn felt the burden of expectations weighing on his mind. He believed he could emerge from the mission with the assets fully intact, but success wasn't guaranteed by any measure.

Numi, one of the crew members, showed Flynn to the crew's quarters below deck.

"You can have this bed here," Numi said. "Showers are at the end of the hall."

Flynn needed a shower to freshen up, but it took a backseat to sleep. He thanked Numi before crashing onto the bed.

He was tired and sore from traversing across Svalbard and desperately needed to get some rest. Despite his level

186 | **R.J. PATTERSON**

of exhaustion, his mind wouldn't stop turning over all the different ways he could eventually get into the country, sneak onto the Russian naval base, and retrieve the seeds. He didn't even entertain the idea that Knudsen was still alive. By now, the Russians had surely dumped her body at the bottom of the sea. Once they made it to port, she'd be nothing but a political liability to them.

Flynn felt regret over her capture. He'd advocated that she get the helicopter in the first place. If she'd been with him and Larsen on dog sleds, she wouldn't be aboard a Russian sub, churning through the Barents Sea toward an imminent death sentence. But such was the unpredictability of war. The move to have her get the Sysselmannen's helicopter was a brilliant stroke of genius until it wasn't.

If they'd been able to secure the seeds, the helicopter would've expedited the process of returning them to the United States. Every day mattered in the looming crisis. But they failed, partially due to her lack of experience in engaging war combatants.

Never show your hand until it's called.

It was an axiom that applied as much to poker as it did to wartime conflicts. She revealed her hand, which she thought was a winning one, only to be trumped by one the Russians held. This setback had left Flynn fighting just to get a seat at the table again. And he realized he was going to have to win with a hand that was equally parts hopeless and toothless. He just needed to figure out a way to make it work.

That's odd.

Flynn wondered why they hadn't started moving yet but dismissed it as a fleeting thought not worth dwelling on. However, their tardiness in heading out to sea made Flynn wonder if they were really taking the time incentive seriously enough.

Instead of sleeping, Flynn stared at the bottom of the bunk above his bed. He needed to talk with Senator Powell and see if he could send some schematics of the Russian naval base as well as tracking of the sub.

He reached into his bag to get his phone and make the call. But the satellite phone wasn't there.

What the—

He sat bolt upright, knocking his head on the frame of the bed above him.

Without hesitating, he emptied all the contents onto the floor and sifted through them.

Nothing.

"Looking for this?" asked a man.

Flynn looked up from the ground where he was methodically sifting through his bag to find it.

It was Larsen, who was holding Flynn's satellite phone.

"What are you—" Flynn started.

"Doing here? Doing with your phone?" Larsen said. "Lots of boring answers."

"Did you take my phone?" Flynn asked.

"Only to make sure the dinghy had a reason to come back to shore and get me. I presumed I could talk my way aboard."

"You were obviously right."

Larsen put the phone in Flynn's hand and nodded.

"You're going to need my help to get Knudsen and the seeds."

Flynn stood up, looking Larsen in the eyes.

"She may not be there when we get there," Flynn said.

"That's a possibility you have to consider."

"I'm very well aware of that fact," Larsen said. "They could have transferred her—"

"They could have killed her."

The cabin fell silent.

"Look," Flynn began, "I'm not trying to be morbid or anything like that, but you have to realize they may look at her as a liability, not an asset. And the minute they come to that realization, they're going to dispose of her, if they haven't already."

"So maybe they have," Larsen said. "It's not going to stop me from asking about her."

"And I'll be with you every step of the way." Flynn clapped and rubbed his hands together. "If she's there, we'll get her."

Larsen nodded.

Flynn pulled out a piece of paper from his backpack and slapped a pencil down on the desk next to it.

"Here is your big chance. Tell me how we're going to get in."

Larsen leaked a wry grin. "That's the easiest part."

CHAPTER 33

BEREZIN CLIMBED ATOP the Severodinsk as the sub glided into the harbor to dock. The Russian military closed the town after sensitive information regarding the fleet stationed there was leaked five years prior. Everything about the naval base became public, resulting in a complete reconstruction of the facility due to the paranoia of President Mirov. He preferred to be shrouded in mystery rather than exposed through transparency. And since he closed ranks, the fate of Russia had taken a gradual climb, both in global public perception and in reality.

Berezin fell in lockstep with all of Mirov's new changes within the Russian military, particularly the naval branch. Russia's maritime operations in the Arctic had always been relatively unknown despite the best espionage efforts by the Americans and other NATO allies. But the brutal storms and icy waters made the Arctic region a non sequitur as it pertained to seafaring activity. By and large, Arctic waters were viewed as important research grounds and little else aside from oil prospecting. Nations aligned through NATO paid little attention to Russia's exercises and exploits in the frigid northern waters.

As a result of the multi-national laissez-faire attitude, Russia had begun to build a powerful fleet around the northern territories of its border. If NATO decided to reverse course in its policy regarding Russia's activities north of the 75th parallel, it would run into fierce opposition that had trained to thrive there.

Berezin found himself at the front of that wave of change within the Russian military, landing a position as the commander of the Severodinsk. It didn't surprise him that he'd been chosen to lead the sensitive operation, handpicked by Mirov himself. The president only wanted the best naval officers in the fleet at the head of potentially the most important mission since the Cold War ended. If successful, Berezin reveled in the idea that Russia would no longer be considered an afterthought on the world stage—it'd be the foremost leader, imposing its will on any country who dared to dissent.

He put his hands on his hips and puffed his chest out, smiling big as a band played the Russian national anthem from the docks. Soaking up the moment, he decided to playfully direct the band until the sub came to a full stop. Several deck hands scurried above board and began securing the vessel while the band continued playing.

Admiral Havelcek greeted Berezin once he reached the dock.

"Excellent work, Commander," Havelcek said. "You have made the entire navy proud."

"It was my pleasure to retrieve the assets, sir."

Havelcek broke into a smile. "We also have a surprise for you. Follow me."

Berezin easily kept pace with Havelcek, who had to stop every few meters to release the officers who paused to salute him. Once they cleared the docks, Havelcek continued toward a large pavilion, which was usually reserved for ceremonies and patriotic speeches before a ship's crew embarked on a six- or nine-month tour. But it was being utilized differently today.

The pavilion was crowded with naval service members, who all stood at attention. Berezin was so stunned by the welcoming party that he didn't initially glance up at the stage. When he did, his eyes widened: President Mirov.

Hands clasped in front of him, Mirov stood smiling on the stage. He rarely let his guard down to show any emotion, but if there was ever a time to do it, it was with the arrival of a Russian sub carrying America's last-known substantial batch of organic corn seed. Berezin glanced over his shoulder at a pair of soldiers carrying the seeds as if they were a trophy of war. And for the most part, they were—the trophies of a war that didn't even require a shot to be fired. Berezin would've deemed it a cold war if America had even been aware that they were at war. The final outcome had been a stroke of genius, one that would return Russia to its rightful place in the world.

Havelcek led Berezin onto a platform, which overlooked all of the other navy members standing at attention below. Mirov turned to Berezin and shook his hand.

"Thank you for your service, commander," Mirov said. "This is how we're going to transform the world and put Russia back on top as the world's pre-eminent superpower. Your role in this operation will not be forgotten."

Mirov winked at Berezin, who smiled big.

A photographer rushed toward them and snapped a picture of the two men shaking hands. It'd likely show up in the Pravda at some point, hailing Berezin as the commander who helped restore Russia through successfully completing his mission.

Berezin took a deep breath and glanced around the large pavilion area. He knew the sailors were there at the request of President Mirov, but they were still looking at him. Despite the glory in the moment, Berezin never aspired to this. Like every other good Russian lad, he simply longed to see his country returned to its place in the world as a superpower. He'd heard the stories as a young boy, stories about what Russia used to be like. But in recent times, the country had suffered a beating, as it pertained to its image—both within the Russian borders and outside of it.

But to see the glory returning—and he had a hand in making it a reality—filled his heart with pride. A tear streaked down his cheek, rolling to a stop just shy of his chiseled jaw line. Berezin surprised himself at how moved he was by the swelling pride of nationalism. This moment was the culmination of all he'd worked for. And in the coming days when the markets began to shift, reflecting the reality that there would be little corn emerging out of the United States later that summer, he'd watch Russia ascend to heights that had only been talked about in recent years, heights that seemed unattainable just a few weeks ago.

He turned stoic as officers from the Severodinsk filed into the pavilion.

Then came Knudsen.

With her hands bound in front of her, she shuffled through the center aisle, keeping her head down.

Mirov found his way to the microphone and edged close to it, pointing at Knudsen.

"That woman right there held our soldiers at gunpoint yesterday, but today she gets justice," Mirov said.

From Berezin's perspective, the Sysselmannen was never a serious threat. But Mirov delivered a narrative that made it sound as if Berezin almost succumbed to Knudsen's power.

"This woman tried to ruin our plans. She tried to ruin our homeland. And she's going to pay for her crimes against this great nation."

The soldiers roared with approval.

Berezin watched as Knudsen labored up the steps and onto the stage. Her escorts nudged her forward.

Mirov wasn't finished. "The world is full of people who want to see us fail. They want to see us punished for actions of long ago that they deem to be unconscionable. But this country and the citizens of this great nation have suffered long enough. People like her have done their best to ruin us. But we will not be stopped. Today, Russia will rise and lead the world."

More raucous applause erupted as two soldiers ushered Knudsen off stage.

The soldiers then began chanting, "Mi-rov, Mi-rov, Mi-rov, Mi-rov."

Mirov reveled in the moment, pumping his fist as he paced around the stage. After a few moments, he held up his hand to quiet the crowd.

"But none of this would have been made possible without the sacrifice of soldiers like Eduard Yolkov and the leadership of men like Commander Nikolai Berezin."

The soldiers all saluted in union at the mention of Berezin's name.

Berezin smiled faintly and remained at attention as Mirov continued his speech.

"As a nation, we have taken steps to ensure that the next generation of citizens from Russia will not be stifled on the global stage like they have in previous years. They will not be disrespected. They will not be mocked or ignored. No, they will be feared and revered. Russia has returned to its former glory—and its light will shine even brighter in this world."

More applause and cheers.

Berezin took a deep breath and relaxed for the first time in months. The pressure every officer and commander in the Russian military had endured over the past few years had sent several good men over the edge. Some cracked and were dismissed, reassigned to Siberia for menial prison duty. Others chose a less graceful exit with a bullet or a rope.

But Berezin felt the pressure lift off of him. He'd been handed a critical assignment and emerged the victor. He couldn't help but break into a big smile as he watched Mirov circle around the stage and pump his fist, signaling the victory every Russian had longed for. The good ole days were no longer a thing of the past—they were about to experience them each day.

Once the ceremony ended, Berezin shook Mirov's hand and posed for a few photos for the Pravda.

Berezin descended the steps when one of his aides approached him.

"Sir, we need to talk," the aide said.

"What is it? Did you take care of the woman?"

"Not exactly."

"Why not? What excuse could you possibly have for defying my orders? I thought I was explicitly clear that she needed to be executed upon arrival."

The aide nodded. "I know, but she asked to speak to one of the officers, who decided it was in our best interest to postpone her execution."

Berezin grunted and rubbed his forehead. "What could she possibly say that would make anyone delay my orders?"

"She said she has information, sir—information about the Americans that you need to hear."

CHAPTER 34

POWELL COULDN'T STOMACH THE NEWS more than five minutes at a time. In a moment where he should have been watching so he could understand the heart of the people's pain and seek to assuage it, he turned away. The contempt and selfishness with which Americans treated their fellow citizens was heartbreaking, if not rage-inducing. The antithesis of everything that made the U.S. admired and revered for centuries around the world had manifested itself in a span of a few days. A country once renowned for helping its neighbors both at home and abroad had transformed into a nation of petulant and greedy brats.

Powell shook his head in disbelief at the report about people stockpiling meat, which was projected to be costly and in short supply in the months ahead. The land of freedom and opportunity had devolved into a place for the opportunistic to be free to gouge their neighbors. Meanwhile, people staged protests in cities both large and small, all full of citizens demanding to take back their government. If Powell was honest with himself, it shouldn't have come as a surprise. America had long since been on the decline, in part thanks to bureaucratic gridlock and political posturing. He and his colleagues on both sides of the aisle had done nothing to ease the plight of middle class Americans. Purposefully or unwittingly, they'd nevertheless fortified a system that rewarded economic behavior benefitting the elite. Instead of fostering generosity and ideas that sought to put the good of the whole ahead of the individual, Powell was left to watch people repeat what got rewarded: sheer selfishness.

He clicked the television off and said a quick prayer under his breath. With the state of affairs on the domestic front reaching levels of pandemonium the country hadn't seen since the early days of the Great Depression, he felt like divine intervention was required.

A knock at his office door snapped him out of his trance, which was quickly leading to a depressed state.

"Come in," Powell said.

One of his aides entered the room.

"Sir, I wanted to give you a heads up before—"

Powell's phone rang, and he held up his index finger. It was his campaign manager.

"Senator, have you heard the news yet?" his manager, Andrew Mann, asked.

"What news?"

"About what's happening in California?"

"What isn't happening in California?"

"This is serious," Mann said.

"I was hoping for a bit of light-hearted news."

"Not happening today—there's a groundswell of support to organize a recall for you. And I don't need to tell you that such a report doesn't bode well for your re-election campaign."

Powell grunted. "We're all screwed anyway. What difference does one more disaster make to me? It's just piling on at this point."

"I thought it was worth giving you a heads up about."

"Thanks. Let me go pour myself a drink and contemplate what to do next," Powell said with a hint of sarcasm.

He hung up and looked at his aide.

"So, how would you like to further ruin my day?" Powell asked.

"I was coming into your office to tell you the exact same thing you just heard?"

"What? That California is organizing a recall effort against me?"

The aide nodded.

"Why did you wait? It would've been nice to know that immediately."

"Sir, I tried and—"

Powell waved him off and spun around in his chair, placing his back to his aide.

"Just leave me alone. I've got less important things to attend to."

"Don't you mean—"

"Get out before I reassign you to coffee detail."

Powell turned the television back on. He didn't even last thirty seconds, so disgusted by the images on the screen that he turned it off and fired his remote across the room.

A recall? What country do we live in? These people are insane.

Powell felt like calling into a radio program and ranting against California voters. It wasn't like he was going to win anyway. His chances re-election just plummeted from eighty percent to less than twenty-five, according to the FiveThir-tyEight.com website. If he was already going to lose, as the website predicted, why not have fun on his way out. Low information voters were the ones who were responsible for putting dozens of irresponsible jerks into Congress anyway. They deserved some of the blame, too, for their ill-informed voting practices, which essentially boiled down to voting for people who promised them things that would supposedly improve their lives. However, the only lives truly being improved were the ruling party in Congress as they cast votes to increase their access to more luxury homes, private islands, and blazing fast corporate jets.

Picking up the phone, Powell dialed Flynn's number.

No answer.

Powell slammed the phone down onto the receiver.

I swear I'm going to explode before this country does.

CHAPTER 35

FLYNN AND LARSEN DUCKED low in the back of an open produce truck headed for Retinskoye, a small fishing village across the inlet from Severomorsk. During his time in the CIA, Flynn had created a lengthy list of helpful contacts around Russia. However, it led nowhere. Larsen, thankfully, had an uncle who lived on the coast of Finland and helped them sneak across the border. He delivered them to a friend who delivered fresh produce all across the region.

"Do you know what they'll do if I get caught?" asked Ruslan Popov, the deliveryman.

"Do you know what will happen if we aren't able to complete this mission?" Flynn responded in an attempt to appeal to the aging Popov's humanity. "The world will be thrown into utter chaos, if it isn't already. You can do a small part to help stop it. I promise that we won't let you get caught."

Popov eventually conceded and seemed proud to be involved in such an important operation. It didn't hurt that Flynn promised to get him ten thousand U.S. dollars either.

Flynn had been unable to reach Senator Powell, but he

did manage to connect with Osborne, giving him an update.

"The senator will be pleased to hear that," Osborne said. "Just don't fail us now."

The cool early morning air nipped at Flynn's nose as he tried to keep his head down. The unfamiliar surroundings in a different part of the world tugged at his curiosity. But he resisted the urge to sit up and gawk. It was a necessary sacrifice if he didn't want Popov to get caught.

After several quick stops in Retinskoye, Popov tapped on the window, signaling the opportunity for them to exit the vehicle.

"You ready?" Flynn asked.

Larsen nodded.

And before Flynn could start a countdown to leap from the moving truck, Larsen jumped first. Flynn sighed and shook his head before catapulting himself over the edge and down a grassy embankment.

The area where Popov suggested they cross the inlet was a wooded portion along the bank. Without any nearby vehicles to catch their suspicious activity, Larsen almost handled the ensuing moments too casually. A man stuck his head out of his car and yelled something at Flynn, drawing his ire.

"Watch what you're doing," Flynn said. "This isn't a game, you know. If they catch us—"

"I know, I know."

"If you know, act accordingly. You're lucky that guy didn't turn around."

Flynn's ears perked up as he heard the whine of a car in reverse heading in their direction.

"Get down."

Larsen dove down, face first in the dirt next to Flynn.

"This is exactly what I'm talking about," Flynn said. "If he reports us, we're finished. And let me tell you, Russian prison is the worst."

Larsen furrowed his brow. "You've spent time in a Russian prison?"

"Not exactly, but I know people who have."

"I'll just take your word for it."

"Good."

After a few tense moments, the sound of a car grinding down into to first gear clattered through the small gulley where they were hiding. The vehicle eased onto the gas and moved down the road.

Flynn poked his head up above the rise they were hiding beneath and noticed that there weren't any other vehicles approaching in either direction.

"We've got to move quickly," he said. "The faster we can get across the water to the base, the better chance we have of saving the Sysselmannen."

"I know you said that you're really after the seeds. She's just a nice bonus for you, isn't she?"

Flynn finished stripping and started to pull his wetsuit on.

"You can judge my motives however you like, but just know one thing: I'm not doing this for the fame or the glory. I'm doing this for the good of the planet—and if I didn't do it, who would?"

Larsen started to pull on his suit as well, ending the contentious debate before it gained any significant steam.

"Do you think we're really going to be able to sneak across the water and reach the base without being seen?" Larsen asked.

"That's the goal."

"So, this is a suicide mission?" Larsen asked.

Flynn shook his head. "I intend on making it out of here alive, as should you. And while I might fear living more based on all the projections about the future, I'm convinced the future holds some hope if we are able to stem the tide."

"And how are we going to do that exactly?"

"By getting the seeds back, of course. It'll strip the Russians of the power they're hoping to gain from this."

"And you trust your own country more than the Russians?"

"Who doesn't?"

Once they finished changing into their wetsuits, they waded into the water, hidden from plain view by the shadows cast by the trees along the banks.

"Do you see the guards in the lookout towers up there?" Larsen asked.

Flynn smiled. "I do—and that's why we're going to make them look the other way when we arrive."

The swim across the inlet took about ten minutes. Flynn identified a location along the shore with some major blind spots. It was all they needed to get ashore and complete the next portion of their mission.

Flynn slithered up the embankment and hid behind a jeep. He pulled out a flash bomb he'd tucked into a plastic bag and carried across the water.

"You really think this is going to work?" Larsen said.

"I don't doubt it for a minute. Just watch and see."

Flynn crouched down and lit the fuse on the bomb, tossing it along the bank. He plugged his ears and counted to five. At five, the explosive device went off, sending the base into a panic. And as Flynn projected, a pair of men headed straight for him.

Flynn and Larsen had crept inside the vehicle and flung the doors open at the right time, sending them to the ground. Snatching up the guards' bodies, Flynn and Larsen dragged them inside the Humvee and redressed, taking their uniforms. In a matter of minutes, the infiltrators were marching around the base as if they belonged there.

"I hope we're not too late," Flynn whispered.

Larsen nodded in agreement. "We won't be. I've got a hunch we'll see Knudsen sooner rather than later.

"I hope you're right," Flynn said.

CHAPTER 36

The Northern Fleet Base
Severomorsk, Russia

KNUDSEN STUMBLED DOWN THE CORRIDOR
after a guard shoved her in the back. Skidding on her stomach before coming to a stop, she slowly pushed herself up
off the ground. Another guard grabbed her collar, yanking
Knudsen to her feet. He placed the butt of his rifle into the
small of her back and thrust her forward again. She kept her
balance.

"Move!" the guard said, preparing to urge her along the
hallway.

She stopped and turned around, holding her bound
hands in front of her.

"Is this really necessary?" she asked.

The guard didn't answer, instead whipping her in the
head with his gun.

"I said move!"

Knudsen had been in some desperate situations in the
past, primarily due to sudden changes in the Arctic weather.
But something felt different. Escaping Mother Nature required skills and equipment, both of which Knudsen had in
abundant supply while traversing across the tundra. But she

possessed neither while taken captive. Yet she needed something else that she deemed inconceivable while moving toward her cell: she needed an ally.

Once she arrived at her cell, one of the guards used his foot to shove her inside before slamming the door shut. He laughed before spitting at her and locking the door.

Knudsen rolled over and sat up. The hard landing on the stone floor resulted in a sharp cut on her knee that bled for a minute while she kept pressure on it with her hand. She stood up and limped to the cot in the corner of the room, sitting down before leaning against the wall and stretching out.

She glanced around at the damp conditions and shook her head, disgusted at her environment.

How did I end up here?

This wasn't her job, nor would anyone expect her to help in the way that she did. But she felt it was necessary—necessary to prove she could do it, necessary to prove her detractors wrong. Then there was a sense of duty. Svalbard was her island, the place she swore to protect. And she'd failed.

She tried to hold back her tears, another task she failed at. Sobbing quietly, she balled up her fist and hit the wall a few times while letting out a few groans.

"Don't be so hard on yourself," a man said. "You probably couldn't have done anything differently."

She got up and limped to the door.

"Who's there?"

"Just another victim of the regime. Pat Dawson, U.S Marine Corps."

She peered into the dark but was unable to see anyone.

"A Marine? Here?"

"Seems crazy, right? I'm just as surprised as you are, trust me."

"How did you—"

"How did I end up here?" he asked. "That's a good question and a long story."

"Apparently, I'm not going anywhere, so you have a captive audience."

Dawson laughed. "That's a fact." He took a deep breath. "Well, if you must know, I'll be happy to tell you."

"Please do tell."

"About five years ago—and that's a rough estimation since I've been rendered unconscious so many times through violence, drugs, and other means—I was on a reconnaissance mission off the northern coast of Russia. Our satellites spotted some strange construction projects going on and sent a team of us to gather intel and report back. One of our guys fired his gun by mistake, alerting the Russian security detail to our presence. Everyone escaped except me."

"And you're still alive."

"If you want to call this alive, sure, I guess. It's more like survival."

"I'm not American, but I doubt it will make much difference."

"Perhaps it will. Just keep your head down and do whatever they tell you to do. Staying alive is your best hope."

"I doubt we have much hope, to be honest. Once the Russians execute the plan I was trying to thwart, they will become an unstoppable machine."

"What's going on out there?" he asked, a small quiver in his voice.

"In short, Russia is creating a global food crisis while

getting rich off its crops. It won't be long until it brings America to its knees."

"Nothing like hunger to coerce people to go along with you. And I can attest to that from firsthand experience."

"Obviously, you've been able to hold out."

"Yeah, but it hasn't been easy."

He held his arm out through the bars in his door next to Knudsen's cell, revealing cuts and scars and burns.

"How do you do it?" she asked. "I mean, how do you survive it all?"

"I just think about the people who love me and want to see me again. I have hope that one day I'll have a chance to go home. Otherwise, I would've given up a long time ago. Being here is no way to live."

Knudsen shared her story with Dawson, explaining how she ended up in the prison. She could tell he had empathy for her.

"So, did you learn anything that could help you get any leverage against them?" he asked.

"Maybe."

"Like what?"

"Plenty of things."

"Such as," Dawson pressed.

Knudsen hobbled back to her cot, wincing as she took each step.

"Can we talk about this later?" she said. "I need to get some rest."

She lay down on her bed and stared at the dark ceiling. Something didn't feel right to her about Dawson's inquisition. He was too forthcoming, too aggressive. She needed to take some time to think and get away from his constant questions.

Interlocking her fingers behind her head, she closed her eyes and tried to review the past twenty-four hours and what went wrong. A more succinct analysis would've been over what went right, which wasn't much.

It might not matter, but at least she knew where the seeds were headed. All she had to do was escape.

CHAPTER 37

Omsk, Russia

GROMOV SPREAD A MAP across his dining room table and weighted it down on all four corners. With a vibrant grin on his face, Gromov clapped his hands before rubbing them together. He called to Irina before putting the finishing touches on his spur-of-the-moment creation. Dotting the map with toothpicks stuck into small pieces of styrofoam, he leaned forward over the table, pleased with his creation.

"What is it, dear?" Irina asked as she glided down the steps.

He rushed over to her at the foot of the stairs, preventing her from seeing around him and into the dining room.

"I'm afraid there's been a change of plans," he said with a dour expression.

"Oh? What is it?"

"We're not going to be able to afford that vacation home now because of some hasty financial moves our son made."

Her face fell, though he could tell she was trying to remain upbeat.

"That's okay. It'd probably just be more trouble than—"

"We not only can afford a vacation home, but we can

also afford an entire island," he said, unable to contain his excitement any longer.

"Wait. Wha—"

"Come with me," Gromov said, leading his wife by the hand into the dining room. "Let me show you."

Her eyes widened as she saw the map, which was dominated by the Aegean Sea.

"Is this what I think it means?"

He nodded. "You can pick out your—our—private island. You said you wanted a place to get away to that was far away from some of our other usual locations. I thought this might be sufficient."

She glanced at the map and then back at him. Without another delay, she hugged him and squealed with delight.

"This is what I always dreamed of," she said. "Can we pick any of these islands?"

Gromov slowly nodded. "Any of them. We can afford them all—and they're all available as of today."

His phone buzzed and he glanced at the screen.

"If you'll excuse me, dear, I need to take this call."

"Certainly, my love."

Gromov stepped into his office and fell into the oversized chair behind his desk.

"I hope you have good news," Gromov said.

"Absolutely, sir. You told me to keep you notified about the progress of the seeds. They will arrive in Omsk in two days."

"Excellent. Thank you for keeping me informed." He paused. "Do you feel it's safe to begin negotiations, especially given everything that's happened recently?"

"I'm sure American farmers will be happy to get their

seeds no matter where they come from."

"Sounds like a yes to me. Thank you."

He sauntered out to the veranda and watched the morning boat activity on the water. He didn't want to throw anything at those people other than money. If he could make it rain money, he would. He closed his eyes for a moment and imagined money falling out of the sky like rain, pelting his house and everyone around him. Even if it was a silly image, it was how he felt.

His phone buzzed again and he smiled.

Maybe instead I should've imagined my phone ringing and money coming out of it.

"Gromov," he said as he answered, excited about the prospect of the call.

"Mr. Gromov," the man began, "I know we don't know each other, but I wanted to connect with you about your offer to help us during this great time of need."

Gromov grunted. "We do know each other. Six years ago, I met you at a conference and suggested we talk. After the conference, your office refused to schedule a meeting for the two of us, telling me each time I called just how busy you were."

"Well, I want to talk now."

"So, what do you want?"

"We wanted to find out if we could potentially borrow your seed-growing facilities for a few urgent projects we have going on. We could pay you handsomely for it."

Gromov tapped his foot on the floor.

"I see, Mr. Wilson. Phillip Wilson, correct?"

"Yes."

"That sounds like an interesting proposition, but let me

get back with you on this. I might have another proposition for you that would prove to be far more lucrative."

Gromov slipped his phone back into his pocket and returned to the dining room, where his wife was standing with an ear-to-ear grin on her face.

"So, did you find an island that suits you?" he asked.

She nodded and rushed toward him, her heels clicking against the marble floor.

"Come with me. I want to show you a video about the island."

"Oh, there's a video."

She grabbed his arm. "There's much more than just a video, but it explains everything." She stopped and stared up at him. "Are you sure we can afford this?"

"I wouldn't be doing this to you if we couldn't. I know how disappointed you get sometimes. When you couldn't buy that twenty-karat diamond or that Italian convertible, the look on your face pained me. It's why I'm working so hard now."

"Don't get too carried away. I don't want my man so focused on work that he forgets about me."

He stroked her cheek with the back of his hand and tucked a few loose strands of hair behind her ear.

"How could I forget about you? You are such a beautiful creation."

She smiled. "Forget the video. I have something else I want to show you."

CHAPTER 38

**The Northern Fleet Base
Severomorsk, Russia**

FLYNN PUT ONE GUARD in a sleeper hold while Larsen knocked another guard out with two punches. They dragged the two bodies into a storage room and proceeded to bind them with duct tape and other materials they scrounged up.

"I need to learn that move," Flynn said. "Two punches?"

"It's a Scandinavian secret," Larsen said. "It's how we subdue wild animals if we are unarmed in the woods."

Flynn studied the edges of Larsen's mouth, which twitched as if they wanted to curl up.

"This sounds more like a tour guide tale than the honest truth."

Larsen broke into a full smile.

"Guilty as charged," he said. "Just a few tricks I learned in a hand-to-hand combat course."

"How long before your guy wakes up?"

Larsen shrugged. "Maybe fifteen minutes? I never timed how long someone stays out."

"Let's get moving then because we don't have much time."

On the ship, Flynn had a chance to download the

schematics of the base and get an idea for where everything was located. The climate-controlled warehouse seemed like the ideal place to store the seeds, though he was certain they wouldn't stay there long. The seeds were also valuable as a commodity, not just as an item held hostage from U.S. farmers. There were also two prisons on the premises; one that was a general holding cell on the main floor of a building in the center, the other that was tucked away in a basement in a facility near the back of the property. According to the blueprints, Flynn made a bet that the Russians would hold Knudsen in the basement. It was far more secure and separated from the rest of the compound, making any type of rescue more challenging, if not impossible.

"I always love a good challenge," Flynn said.

"Me, too, as long as there's a way I can overcome it."

"But first things first. We need to secure the seeds."

Flynn and Larsen strode across the grounds toward the warehouse. Once there, a guard seated at a desk asked them what their business was.

"General Berezin asked us to pick up the seeds and ready them for transport," Flynn explained in his near flawless Russian accent. .

"Right this way, sir," the guard said as he glanced at the ranking insignias on Flynn's and Larsen's jackets.

He led them down a short corridor that opened up into a larger warehouse. Flynn noted all the surface-to-air missiles along with heavy artillery. For a navy base, he noted that it seemed more than capable of defending itself against all measures of attacks.

The guard took them to a corner and gestured toward a large wooden box.

"I believe what you're looking for is in there."

He unlocked the box and opened the lid.

Flynn and Larsen knelt down in front of the box and began looking at the contents intently. There were several maps of Svalbard and the Sysselmannen's gun—and two large bags of seeds. Flynn picked up the bag and studied it closely. It contained something other than the heirloom seeds. He cut open the bag and shoved his hand inside, pulling out a fistful of seeds.

Holding up the seeds to the guard, he glared at him.

"What is the meaning of this?" Flynn asked.

"I—I don't understand," the guard stammered.

"Someone has played you for a fool," Flynn said as he flung the seeds to the ground. "These are not the corn seeds that we brought back from the Arctic. These are—I don't even know what these are."

The guard cowered back before standing upright.

"Sorry, sir. I will find out about this immediately."

Flynn sneered. "Don't bother. I'll do it myself."

They hustled out of the warehouse, heading across the compound.

"Where does that leave us?" Larsen asked.

"Not in a good position."

"How did you know the seeds were compromised? Do you have a background in botany?"

Flynn smiled. "No, but I know enough to understand the difference between seeds that have been coated and seeds that haven't been. Heirloom seeds in the vault would never have a protective coat on them."

"So, now what?"

"Let's go save Knudsen. She might know something."

Larsen walked swiftly to keep pace with Flynn. "You didn't think this was going to be easy, did you?"

Flynn shook his head. "No, but I didn't expect a monkey wrench in our plans so soon?"

"A monkey what?"

"Never mind. Just follow my lead in here."

Flynn and Larsen entered the building with the basement prison on the edge of the compound. They told the two guards at the front desk that General Berezin requested their presence in the main building and to see him immediately. Flynn's high-ranking uniform mitigated any protest, however slight it could have been. The soldiers dashed out the door and Flynn and Larsen remained frozen for a few seconds as they watched the men head toward the headquarters building.

Flynn looked at his watch. "We've got five minutes to find her and get her out before they come back or radio to someone that something is wrong."

"Well, let's get moving then."

Flynn grabbed the building's key ring sitting on the desk and began making rounds. Once they reached the steps downstairs, they needed a key to get in. It took about half a minute for Larsen to find the right one and jam it into the doorknob.

As they ran into the prison area, they found cell after cell of bedraggled captives. But they were all men, except one.

"Knudsen?" Flynn said, straining to see into the dimly lit cell. "Is that you?"

"Flynn?" came the response.

"Open the door. Open the door," Flynn said, rushing Larsen.

But as the woman moved toward him in the light, he realized it wasn't her. It was Lexie Martin, who he'd last seen in Russia in the Ural Mountains while trying to take down the Kuklovod.

"Wait. What are you doing here? I thought—"

"It's a long story," she said. "Here to save the damsel in distress again?"

"She saved me once so I figured I should return the favor."

She laughed. "You'll go to great lengths to repay your debts to beautiful women."

"Come on," Larsen said, tugging on Flynn's shirt. "We've got to go. You can have a reunion later. We need to get the Sysselmannen."

Flynn lingered for a few seconds before dashing down the corridor behind Larsen.

"What? You're just going to leave me here now?" she called out.

Flynn breathed heavy as he kept pace with Larsen.

"Where are you taking me?" Flynn asked between breaths.

"I found a—a door," Larsen said, panting. "It's near the—the back and it's small. But I think—I think I hear someone in there. But we've got to hurry. We've only got—only got three minutes."

They came to the door, and Larsen inspected the lock. The keyhole was oddly shaped and required a shorter key.

"There you go," Larsen said as he jammed the key inside the lock and turned it to the left.

The door swung open, and the two men rushed inside.

A dim lighting system kept the place almost completely

shrouded in the dark. Flynn heard running water and looked down to see a small stream trickling between the cracks in the cobblestone floor.

"What is this place?" Larsen said. "Looks like where you might hold a séance."

"Or a prisoner you don't very much like," Flynn said. "Knudsen? Are you in here?"

"Flynn is that you?" came the soft reply.

"Knudsen!" Larsen cried as he rushed into the dark.

"What are you doing here, Larsen?" she asked. "I didn't think you'd—"

"You didn't think I was going to let this Yank have all the glory, now did you?" Larsen said.

Flynn rushed into her cell and helped her get her arm around him. Larsen helped on the other side as he and Flynn assisted Knudsen in gaining her balance outside the cell and walking.

"Are you hurt?" Flynn asked.

"A little, but I can make it. If I can survive a polar bear attack, this is nothing, right?" she said dryly.

After they squeezed through the small opening and back toward the main prison area, Flynn looked at his watch.

"We've only got two minutes, so we've got to make this quick," he said.

They returned to the main corridor of the general prison area, this time met with a few angry stares.

"Where the hell are you going, Flynn?" Lexie said. "You can't just leave me here."

"Sorry, Lexie," Flynn said as he looked over his shoulder. "There's nothing I can do to help you right now."

He noticed his companions had stopped. Flynn glanced

ahead and saw three gunmen directly in their path with their rifles trained on them.

"He's right, Lexie," the center guard said. "There's nothing he can do to help you, but maybe you can keep him company in the box."

"That's okay," Lexie answered. "I'll stay out here."

The guard walked up to her cell and spit at her.

"Not another word—and no dinner for you tonight."

The guard placed his hands behind his back and then turned toward his three captors.

"Looks like it's going to be crowded in the box tonight."

CHAPTER 39

Friday, May 4

COMMANDER BEREZIN PREPARED TO EXIT his office when his secretary alerted him to an incoming call. He glanced at the clock, already in a hurry to make it to the train station in the next half hour with the asset secured for transport. Exasperated, he exhaled.

"Put him through," Berezin said as he returned to his office and sat down to answer the call.

"President Mirov, to what do I owe this honor?"

"I wanted to call and congratulate you on accomplishing such a great feat. I know it couldn't have been easy to complete this last portion of your mission, but you will be rewarded for your skillful retrieval."

Berezin tried to downplay the president's effusive praise.

"It's what any good soldier would have done, sir."

"But you're not just any soldier—you're a commander. And you seem to have a firm grip on your troops while being able to assess each person's strengths and weaknesses. That's what real leadership is all about."

"Thank you for your kind words, sir. I appreciate you saying that."

"Next week at our council meeting, I'm going to recommend a promotion for you."

"A promotion?"

"Yes, I think it time for you to move up the chain of command."

"I'm grateful, but I—"

"I'll hear no protests, Commander," Mirov said. "You deserve it."

"Thank you."

"Mother Russia thanks you."

Mirov hung up, and Berezin did likewise. However, the news almost paralyzed him. He'd never dreamed he would rise to the ranks of a commander. But a general? That was only one step from entering politics. Yet, nothing was guaranteed.

Berezin glanced at the clock on his wall as the seconds ticked by. He didn't have to personally get on the train and deliver the goods to Gromov. But he couldn't risk such an important task being entrusted to anyone else—especially for what Gromov offered to pay him for the seeds.

Berezin grabbed his hat and coat and hustled out the door.

***

AT THE TRAIN STATION, Berezin received special accommodations in the sleeper car and requested that his cargo be placed in the room. However, one of the baggage handlers informed him that his box was too large to get into his cabin.

"Where are you placing this cargo then?" Berezin asked.

"Don't worry, Commander. It will be safe in the back with the rest of the cargo."

Berezin growled. "It's not leaving my sight, so show me where the cargo hold is."

The man shrugged and led Berezin to the back of the train where all the extra cargo was stored. Berezin surveyed the area. It looked secure enough, but he wasn't inclined to leave anything to chance. Too many things could go wrong—and some already had. If it hadn't been for some astute guards, the two men who'd infiltrated his base would be fleeing the country with his cash cow. He knew better than to be played a fool twice. He took an extra blanket from a tall stack and made a comfortable seat for himself right next to the box.

"I can bring a cot in here for you if that's what you want, Commander," the handler said.

"This will do just fine. When you've slept on the cold stony ground while on a mission, this is plenty sufficient."

The handler shrugged and returned to the main passenger cabins.

Berezin dug into his pocket and fished out a small bottle of vodka. He'd been waiting to break it open since the moment he took the seeds into his hand. After staring at the bottle for a few seconds, he put it away.

"Patience. Patience," he said aloud to himself.

He wouldn't truly celebrate until the train left the station, but even that seemed like it might be a bit premature. Until he had the money in his account from Gromov, everything he was doing was an exercise in discipline and detail.

He closed his eyes and saw the numbers on the screen of his computer. He'd never have to get on a submarine again and do the president's bidding. In a few days, he'd be the commander of a ship that would go wherever he deemed it desirable to sail. No more orders from anyone about anything.

Just a three-day train ride.

CHAPTER 40

The Northern Fleet Base
Severomorsk, Russia

OLEG DUDNIK DISMISSED the other guards outside the cell and insisted he could handle all the extra duties. The tray full of food wobbled as he insisted that they take leave from their shift. His partner would be there any minute, and there wasn't reason for them to sit around and wait for him to get there.

"The protocol is that we wait for two guards to relieve us of our duty," one of the guards seated at the table said. "One is not acceptable."

"One is enough for me," the other guard said. "I've got a wife and kids to get home to."

"And you?" Dudnik asked the remaining guard.

"I sleep on the couch."

Dudnik laughed and threw some money at the guard.

"Then get your rubles worth and go drinking before you go home."

The guard slowly stood up, pushing his chair backward with the back of his knees.

"I hope no one finds out about this. If so, it'll be—" the guard said before making a throat slashing gesture with his hand "—for the both of us."

"Don't worry," Dudnik said. "I have seen far too many of those around here to want to see another one."

"Good. Be safe."

Dudnik nodded and sat down at the desk. He watched the men carefully, waiting for them to completely disappear from his field of view before taking any action. The food on the tray in front of him was getting cold, but he didn't care—and neither would its intended recipients. It's not like they would ever eat it or think that they missed it.

He chambered a round in his pistol and strode toward the main cell block.

The prisoners either derided him or begged for the food. On top was a steak along with potatoes and a salad. To Dudnik, the meat looked dry and the potatoes overcooked. But to the men drooling over the slab of meat, it appeared as if it were a gourmet dinner that had been prepared by one of the country's top chefs.

Once he reached the door leading to the chamber separated from the rest of the cell block, he twisted the key slowly and unlocked the door. The door's squeaky hinges could hardly be heard over the men still calling for Dudnik to toss them the meal on his tray. Dudnik stopped before he entered and slid the food to the man in the corner who'd yet to utter a word, much less a sound.

"Thank you, sir," the man said as he dragged the tray beneath the door, individually lifting each piece of food over the bar and into his cell.

Dudnik nodded knowingly and crouched low to enter the small cell. He wasted little time in opening the first cell door he came to. Without hesitating, Dudnik put two rounds in the prisoner before he proceeded to collapse to the ground.

He moved to the next cell and jammed his key in the lock before turning it to the left. Dudnik swung the door open and gestured for the prisoners to exit.

At first they seemed hesitant, suspect of his motives.

"What are you doing?" Knudsen brazenly asked.

"That prisoner was a plant, designed to extract information from you," he answered. "Now, we don't have much time. We have to move quickly."

The three prisoners crouched low to exit the special cell before heading to the main block. A chorus of jeers echoed throughout the room.

"You'll all be next," Dudnik announced, which quieted down the crowd.

"Make sure she gets out," Flynn said, pointing at Lexie Martin.

"They're all going to get out," Dudnik said. "Every last one of them, but not until you escape."

They hustled up the stairs and onto the first floor where Dudnik had guard uniforms waiting for each of them along with a packet of papers and a set of keys to help them escape the base.

"Tuck your hair up underneath your hat," Dudnik said to Knudsen. "You'll be fine."

"Why are you doing this?" Knudsen asked.

"It is simple, really. I hate Commander Berezin. He murdered a man who served him loyally and put himself in harm's way to get those seeds. But he didn't want to pay Yolkov, though Berezin will make millions. It was disgusting."

"And you'd betray your own country?" Flynn asked.

Dudnik hung his head, refusing to look Flynn in the eyes.

"My country has betrayed me."

Flynn, Larsen, and Knudsen grabbed their military attire and rushed into the restrooms to change. In less than two minutes, they all emerged, appearing as sharp Russian soldiers.

"No one will suspect a thing," Dudnik said as he flashed a thumbs-up sign.

Flynn nodded imperceptibly.

"So where are the seeds?" Flynn asked.

"You don't need to worry about the seeds," Dudnik said. "There isn't much time for you to escape."

"Without those seeds, the world is going to be thrown into chaos in the coming years. People are going to die from hunger. There won't be enough food to go around. That's what this is all about."

Dudnik sighed. "I don't think you'll be able to catch them now, but they're about to board a train headed south. I think it is scheduled to leave in about thirty minutes."

"Can we make it in time?" Flynn asked.

"If we hurry," Dudnik said as he grabbed a pair of keys off the desk.

"We?" Flynn asked.

"I'm coming with you. Just give me a second."

They all watched Dudnik set the timer for a charge on the handle of the door leading into the prison area. He pulled a lever, releasing all the doors.

"None of those people really deserve to be there," he said. "Plus, it'll be quite the diversion."

"Where to now?" Flynn asked.

"Follow me. There's a base jeep out back."

***

FLYNN FOLLOWED DUDNIK outside with Larsen and Knudsen trailing close behind.

"Do you think this is going to work?" Knudsen whispered to Flynn as she tugged her hat down tight across her face.

"It's our best bet at the moment," Flynn said as he glanced at the gun holstered around his waist. "At least we have a fighting chance."

Dudnik climbed behind the wheel of a jeep and drove toward the exit. He handed a guard a few documents and waited. After studying the papers and glancing at all the occupants in the vehicle, the guard waved them through.

Moments after they turned onto the main road, Flynn heard gunshots in the background.

"What do you think that is all about?" Knudsen asked.

"My diversion," Dudnik said. "It worked. Oh, and I almost forgot. Look in my bag."

Flynn reached into the bag resting between the two front seats.

"What am I looking for?"

"Your satellite phone. I found it in the guard's desk."

Flynn finally laid his hand on it, pulling it out.

"How'd you know this was mine?"

Dudnik laughed softly. "I know the difference between Russian and American technology."

Flynn proceeded to dial a number.

"Flynn," said the voice on the other line. "You're still alive."

Flynn was torn between giving a warm greeting to his

former CIA colleague Todd Osborne or scolding him for giving his name out to Senator Powell.

"Osborne, so are you," Flynn said, opting for the more ambiguous response. "How the heck are you?"

"Cut the bullshit," Osborne said. "I know you're in trouble."

"More like was in trouble, but I've somehow managed to navigate my way out of it—no thanks to you."

"Look, I'm sorry. DHS tied my hands and Powell acted like he was your primary go-between," Osborne said. "Please cut me a little slack."

"Maybe. But you're going to owe me big time when I return."

"That's what I like to hear. You're coming home."

Flynn sighed. "But not just yet."

"How can I help?"

"I need everything you know about a Russian commander named Nikolai Berezin. We need to take him out if we ever intend to get those seeds back."

CHAPTER 41

ON THEIR WAY TO THE TRAIN STATION, Flynn and Dudnik went over their plan. Flynn conceded that it wasn't the greatest, but it had the best chance of working in regards to getting them on the train. If they achieved their initial goal, the rest of the operation's success would hinge on their ability to execute. Dudnik jammed his foot on the accelerator pedal in an effort to arrive before Berezin departed with the seeds and created more insurmountable odds.

"Are you sure this is our best opportunity for getting onto that train?" Knudsen asked. "I'm not too interested in returning to a Russian prison."

"You're not going back," Flynn said. "Trust me."

"That's what my ex-husband said before he stabbed me in the back," she said.

Flynn eyed her closely. "I'm not your ex-husband."

A few minutes later, they pulled into the train station. The conductor called for the final boarding.

"That's our cue," Dudnik said.

Flynn and Larsen dragged Knudsen in tow as they rushed toward the platform.

"We're ready to board," Flynn said.

The ticket taker looked them up and down.

"Not like that, you aren't," he said. "Those shoes are scuffed and your hair is a mess. Don't you have any sense of decorum? What are they teaching people in the military these days?"

Dudnik shoved his credentials in the face of the train employee.

"Stop giving them a hard time," Dudnik said.

"Very well then. Please board," the ticket taker said as he stepped back and allowed them passage onto the train.

The new quartet boarded and requested a free cabin. One of the train employees led them to an unoccupied room and told them that they could stay there for the next two legs of the trip.

"I'm not sure how long you intend to be on this train, but on the third day, someone has this room booked," he said.

"We won't be here that long," Dudnik said.

They all exhaled a sigh of relief once the train employee left the room.

"Do you always get such great upgrades in the Russian military?" Flynn asked.

"When possible," Dudnik quipped with a wry grin.

"Well, we're less concerned with enjoying these nice accommodations and more concerned with snagging the seeds so we can escape across the border with them," Flynn said.

"That's—how do you say it—easier said than done?"

Flynn chuckled. "You've got the phrases down, but do you know what it means?"

"It means we're going to have to make one hell of an effort to pry Berezin's hands off the seeds if you intend to reclaim them."

"We're prepared to do whatever is necessary," Larsen said.

"In that case, I know where he's likely hiding them," Dudnik said.

"On board?" Knudsen said.

Dudnik nodded. "Based on the security situation, there's no doubt that they're on board. However, that doesn't make them easy to obtain."

"So what do you suggest?" Flynn asked.

"If we isolate Berezin and the seeds, I think we'll have the best chance at getting them back."

"And when do you think this should occur?" Knudsen asked.

"Just outside of Medvezhyegorsk. It's a rural area with plenty of opportunities to escape, not to mention that it's not that far from the Finnish border. Once you escape over the border, you'll be free."

***

EVERY MEMBER OF FLYNN'S TEAM enjoyed a long nap as the train headed south. But it wasn't out of exhaustion as much as it was out of necessity. The hours ahead would prove to be challenging, if not extremely taxing. They needed all the rest they could get before engaging in a strenuous task to escort the seeds out of enemy territory and across the Russian border. Anything less than success would be an utter failure for the rest of the world. Thousands, if not hundreds of thousands, of lives were at stake.

Several hours into the trip after everyone had fallen asleep, Dudnik awakened Flynn by shaking his leg.

"It's time," Dudnik said.

Flynn woke up the rest of his team and told them to get

ready quickly so they could do what they came to Russia to do.

Within minutes, they were all armed and prepared to engage Berezin.

"Do we all understand what we're doing?" Flynn asked.

Everyone nodded.

"Let's do this."

The sun was still up, but it was sinking fast on the horizon. Flynn glanced at his watch. It was nearly ten o'clock. In a few more minutes, it'd be practically dark.

One by one, they filed out of the cabin and headed toward the back of the train near the cargo hold.

"Are you ready?" Flynn asked Dudnik.

He nodded. "Please avenge this bastard."

Flynn, Knudsen, and Larsen climbed atop the cargo car as stealthily as possible—and waited.

Leaning over the edge, Flynn watched as Dudnik finagled the connector loose, freeing the cargo hold and the caboose from the rest of the train.

Berezin stumbled out of the car and stared in disbelief as he realized what was happening. He began cursing at Dudnik.

"You are not a patriot," Dudnik screamed at him. "You're just a common thief."

Berezin sneered at Dudnik, who tried to scramble back inside once Berezin began firing at the soldiers who'd been in his keep. Berezin unloaded several shots in the direction of Dudnik, the last of which hit him in the head. Dudnik tumbled over the edge and rolled into a ditch.

Flynn wished he hadn't seen it, but it was an image he couldn't shake. Dudnik's body was still rolling down an embankment as they continued on, albeit at a much slower speed than before.

Flynn took a deep breath and tried to calm down.

"It's about control, not rage," he said aloud.

"What did you say?" Larsen asked him.

"Never mind. Are you ready?"

Larsen nodded.

"Are you ready?" he asked as he looked at Knudsen.

She nodded.

"Follow my lead."

CHAPTER 42

SENATOR POWELL STARED at the report on his desk and sighed. Another polling service conducted an overnight survey and found that more than eighty percent of likely voters would prefer to see Powell removed from Congress.

"Are these people insane?" Powell asked aloud. "I'm the only one here looking out for their best interest yet they want to cast me aside as if I'm the one targeting them."

A knock on his door halted his rant.

"Is everything all right in there, Senator?" his secretary asked.

"I'll be fine. Nothing to worry about."

"Okay. I just heard you talking and I—"

"Just get back to work."

"Yes, sir."

Powell felt himself slowly descending into depression. Almost daily, some new disaster was erupting and challenging his leadership resolve, not to mention his sanity. Accusations of impropriety, corruption, and fraud haunted him as he tried to help the country avoid an impending fiscal meltdown, the likes of which it had never seen. Even the Great Depression was sure to be tame in comparison to what was coming. Skyrocketing food prices, devaluation of the dollar, unstable homeland security, and the rebirth of a superpower in Russia that was led by a ruthless leader—all the ingredients necessary to cause a revolution at best, a world war at worst.

Trying to get his mind off the doom hovering over him, Powell tried to read some of his emails. His position as head of the U.S. Senate Committee on Agriculture, Nutrition and Forestry required that he rule on a few requests, a task he'd neglected in recent days. He'd grown so tired of all the bureaucracy related to his work that he began to wonder if the recall vote was a blessing instead of a curse. Maybe outside of Congress, he could actually do what he wanted to do from the moment he set foot on Capitol Hill: Make a difference in the lives of people. But that desire had been usurped by an unquenchable thirst for power and wealth. Somewhere along his journey, the glittering allure of money and authority arrested his attention. It wasn't all bad at first. When he first began to experience the subtle temptations, Powell resisted, holding fast to his foundational principles and morals. But the more he tried to hold back, the stronger the desire became—until he decided to taste it.

At first, Powell's transition seemed nearly imperceptible, both to himself and to outside observers. He justified taking a luxurious trip to the Bahamas with Fenestra execs as a way to gain a deeper understanding about the issues related to the senate committee that he oversaw. But then he came to realize that bi-annual trips were less and less about discussions dealing with pertinent issues to a business dealing in his realm of authority and more and more about extravagant decadence. However, he stopped caring.

If Powell chose to be honest about the situation, the end

of his time in office was imminent. He'd taken his last junket. He'd tasted his last five-hundred-dollar bottle of champagne. He'd dipped his toes in the waters off some CEO's private island for the last time. It was over—and he hated to see access to such finer things vanish under the weight of a campaign building momentum daily to oust him.

He paced around the room and looked at himself in the mirror, the lines around his eyes starting to permanently crease his skin. In such a short time by Washington's standards, he'd charged into Washington on a crusade to change everything that was wrong with the government only to fall victim to it and eventually embrace the system, a system that was broken for everyone except those who benefitted from it. And the list of benefactors was a short one.

His secretary buzzed him, and he sat down in his chair before answering.

"Yes?"

"The president's office just called and said the president wants to speak with you. It's line one."

"Thank you," Powell said as he pressed the button for line one. "This is Senator Powell."

"Please hold for the president, sir."

A few seconds of silence followed by a click preceded the president's voice.

"Dan, how the heck are you?" the president asked.

"I've been better, sir."

"Well, I hear there's a recall effort underway back home for you. Just hang in there. It'll blow over."

"I'm not so sure about that, sir. It seems like it's only gaining steam."

The president chuckled. "Trust me. It'll be gone before

you know it, especially when I call you out for being the hero in saving this country from a further food crisis."

Powell was quiet.

"Dan? You still there?"

Powell glanced skyward. "Still here."

"Did you hear what I said?"

"Not sure how that's going to turn out for me, but I hope you're right."

"Well, you're the one running point on this mission with the former CIA operative to retrieve the corn seeds, am I right?"

"I wouldn't call my position running point, but I have been able to help him some."

"And how's that coming along?"

Powell took a deep breath. "I wish I knew. I haven't heard from him in several days. I can only hope he's still alive and working hard to secure the seeds for us."

"That's not the news I wanted to hear. Remember, I've got my big address from the Oval Office tomorrow evening, and I wanted to find out if you've got something I can insert into my speech that would help assure the people that we're going to get through this."

"At this point, you can't make those assurances in good faith."

The President pounded his fist on the table. "Then make sure I can do it in good faith, then."

"I'll give you an update tomorrow, sir."

"Excellent. I'll be looking forward to it."

Powell interlocked his fingers behind his head as he stood up and paced around his office. The President's latest request almost made him laugh, but mostly because Powell couldn't make such assurances even if he was sitting on the seeds in his basement at his house.

The only thing Powell could do with the remaining shred of integrity he had left was to assure the president that he'd do his best to prevent such atrocities from ever happening again. But even that felt like a weak promise, if not impossible.

He dialed Phillip Wilson's number and waited for the Fenestra CEO to answer his call.

"Senator, I appreciate the call. How are you?" Wilson asked.

"I'm guessing that I'm the same as you, which means we're both going about our day with about eight less shots of scotch than we need."

Wilson politely laughed. "Well, Senator, I'm afraid my day's not going that poorly. I'm only going about with one less shot than I'd prefer."

"So you started drinking early then?"

"OK, Senator, I appreciate the humorous banter, but I've got a company to run. Would you mind telling me about the nature of your call?"

Powell exhaled slowly. "Not on the phone. We need to meet in person."

"Great. You name the place and I'll be there."

"Are you in town right now?"

"As a matter of fact, I am. I've got a meeting with one of our board members in the morning."

"Good. Why don't you come over to my house this evening for some scotch and straight talk? Say sevenish?"

"Sounds like a plan to me."

"I'll text you my address."

"Looking forward to it, Senator."

Powell hung up and stared out the window, contemplating what the following evening would look like. It wouldn't be pretty, but he was prepared for the consequences.

Powell pulled open the bottom drawer in his desk and grabbed a flask, setting it to the side on the floor. Digging farther into the back, he felt for the wooden grip, one that felt cold in his hand. He pulled it out and set it on the table.

There was another way out of the mess he faced.

CHAPTER 43

BEREZIN WATCHED DUDNIK'S BODY roll down into the ravine. It was the first time he'd ever been amused at the death of one of the men under his command. He chuckled and blew a kiss in the direction of Dudnik's body.

Bastard deserved it.

He grabbed the rail on the platform outside of the car to steady himself. Clicking along at a slower pace, he wondered how long it would be before the rest of the train noticed it had lost a car.

At least I've still got the seeds.

He yanked on the door to return to the cabin and find his phone. The engineers still hadn't noticed. Berezin needed to let someone know sooner than later before another train made a mess of the situation and collided with the stray car.

As he went to reach for his phone, it slid toward the front of the car—and he along with it. While Berezin couldn't be completely sure, it seemed like a braking mechanism had been activated. Puzzled by this development, he regained his balance and walked outside to investigate.

Once he stepped through the door and onto the platform outside, a pair of boots flew at his face with extreme force. The heels bashed him in the face, sending him back-

247

ward against the car.

Berezin closed his eyes tightly and opened them again just in time to see a right cross coming toward him. His face suffered the brunt of the blow, spinning him to the side. He tried to regain his composure and his balance before he got hit from the left.

"Do you know who I am?" he screamed as he tried to regain his bearings.

"We sure do, Commander," a man's voice said before another punch from the right rattled him in the face.

"I said do you know who I am?"

Another punch sent Berezin stumbling across the platform.

He turned around and locked eyes with the man standing in front of him.

"And who are you?" Berezin asked.

"I've come to take back something you stole?" the man said.

Berezin chuckled. "I'm not a common thief, so apparently, you don't know who I am. I am Commander—"

"Titles don't impress me," the man said. "Now, where are the seeds?"

Berezin squinted and rubbed his brow.

"Seeds? I'm not sure I know what you're talking about?"

"Don't play dumb with me. You know exactly what I'm talking about."

Berezin chuckled and shook his head.

"I'm afraid I don't."

The man rushed toward Berezin and delivered a fierce body blow, forcing him to double over.

Berezin remained bent over, unable to stand upright,

while the man joined Berezin. He put his arm around Berezin and leaned over him.

"Where are the seeds?"

Berezin remained defiant. "I don't know what you're talking about."

A knee to the stomach followed by two punches to the face and Berezin's head was spinning.

"This is the last time I'm going to ask you," the man said. "Where are the seeds?"

"Even if I knew, you think I'd tell you?" Berezin said.

"Hold him while I search the car," the man said to his accomplice standing on the other side of the platform.

The other man was far less delicate in dealing with Berezin, grabbing his hair and yanking him toward the edge of the platform.

"It's not so easy to be tough when you're not in control."

Berezin sneered at the man before attempting a punch. The man grabbed Berezin's hand.

"Perhaps you need a lesson in manners."

Berezin spit in the man's face.

A few seconds later, Berezin watched the other man emerge from the cabin holding two bags of seeds.

"Never mind, Commander. We found what we came here for."

With the car almost fully stopped on the tracks, Berezin realized he needed to make a move or else he'd see his fortune likely disappear, not to mention his ranking.

Berezin lunged for the man's gun and wrestled it away from him. The other man dropped the seeds and drew his gun, creating a standoff.

"Well, well. Look what we have here," Berezin said. "Looks like those seeds aren't so important after all."

Berezin kept his gun trained on the man holding the weapon.

"There are two ways we can go about this. I can shoot both of you and you can shoot me and we all die in a bloody heap on the tracks. Or you can put your gun down and I won't kill either of you and promise to make sure your life in prison is as comfortable as possible. So, which is it going to be?"

The man with the gun lowered his weapon.

"Good choice," Berezin said. "Now, if you don't mind, please put those bags back in the cabin here."

He watched as the man he'd disarmed placed the bags inside.

"That's it. Nice and easy," Berezin said.

Once the second bag had been tossed inside, Berezin smiled.

"So, who wants to go first?"

Neither of the men said anything as they both furrowed their brows.

"I know, I know. I said that I'd let you live, but I lied," Berezin said before breaking into laughter.

He laughed so heartily that he didn't have time to react when a pair of legs descended from the roof of the car and wrapped around his head. Berezin buckled beneath the weight, his arms flailing.

That's when one of the men rushed toward Berezin and disarmed him.

Berezin stood mouth agape, trying to grasp at what just happened.

How could I be so careless? Three of them?

As reality settled on the Russian commander, he eyed the woman closely.

"I know you," Berezin said. He recognized her as the Sysselmannen from Svalbard.

"But I bet you don't even know my name, do you?" she said.

He shook his head. "I know who you are though."

"You didn't treat me with respect, and I'm not exactly inclined to return the favor," she said.

"You will regret this."

"Actually, you're going to be the one who regrets everything you did."

One of the other men protested.

"Kari, this is not the kind of person you are," he said. "Put the gun down."

She trained her gun on Berezin, refusing to drop it.

"Put the gun down. We don't have to kill him."

She glared at Berezin. "I think we do."

"He's not worth it. We got what we came for. The damage has been done."

Berezin watched as she eyed him carefully.

"What if he comes after us?" she said.

"I'm sure he will, but it won't matter."

She lowered her gun and exhaled—and Berezin with her.

Berezin looked at his hands, which had been holding onto the railing with a death grip, whitening his knuckles. The blood rushed back into his hands—and the rest of his body.

"That's the way," one of the men said. "All the way down."

By the time the gun fell downward, Berezin reached for her.

"Kari! Your gun!" one of the men yelled.

She withdrew her arms and spun around to avoid any extracurricular confrontation. But it was too late. Berezin had grabbed her arm and yanked her toward him.

She didn't hesitate as she spun before filling his head and chest with several bullets. Berezin collapsed onto the platform in a mess as the blood formed a pool and dripped slowly onto the track below.

"Please," Berezin said as he rolled over, "make it quick."

The woman squeezed off two more shots.

Berezin barely flinched after the second shot.

He was gone.

CHAPTER 44

A FULL MOON LOOMED large on the horizon and battled with the last rays of dusk for control of the night. Flynn and Larsen both lugged a bag of the seeds on their shoulders as they climbed off the cargo car and struck out across the grassy field. The train had long since disappeared around the bend, and Flynn hoped it didn't return until they'd managed to reach the tree line about a kilometer away.

"Did you grab his wallet?" Flynn asked Larsen.

Larsen held it up. "There's plenty of cash in here."

"Good," Flynn said. "We're going to need it if we intend to make it to the border alive."

He glanced at Knudsen who was a few steps behind them. With her arms crossed and head down, she remained silent as she trudged through the field. They'd all found some clothes in the car and changed, but Flynn was surprised at how attractive Knudsen was when she wasn't bundled up in Arctic gear, beaten badly in prison, or sporting military attire. Then he saw a pack of cigarettes and a lighter in her hand.

"Of all the things to take from the car, you found a pack of smokes?" Flynn asked.

"I only do it when I'm stressed out."

"Well, I'm a lot less stressed out now because of you, Kari. You saved our ass back there," Flynn said. "I can't thank you enough."

She didn't look up. "It's been a while since I killed someone."

"He had it coming to him," Larsen said.

"Makes no difference to me. You never feel good about taking another person's life."

Flynn slowed his pace enough to walk in step with her. He put his arm around her, squeezing her shoulder a couple of times.

"You're a good woman, Kari Knudsen. Just remember that."

"As much as I wanted to kill him for all that he did to me—or threatened to do to me—I still don't feel great about it."

Flynn nodded. "You don't have to feel great about it, but you did what needed to be done, for us and for this mission, a mission you never planned to be on. But you're a survivor and a fighter. And that's why you're here and that piece of garbage Berezin isn't."

She lifted her head and nodded imperceptibly. She pulled out a cigarette and lit it.

"I did owe that son of a bitch something, didn't I?" she said, forcing a smile before exhaling a mouthful of smoke.

"He never knew what hit him," Larsen said.

They plodded along for a few more minutes until they reached the tree line and went deep into the woods.

"So, what's the plan now?" Knudsen asked. "Are we just going to march all the way to Finland with these things?"

"I'm hoping we find some civilization out here soon and

get resourceful enough to get us across the border," Flynn said.

"Any suggestions?" Knudsen asked.

Flynn saw something up ahead and broke into a jog, followed by a sprint.

"I've got an idea," he yelled over his shoulder. "Come on."

Once they reached the top of a rise in a small clearing, Flynn saw small plumes of smoke billowing from a cabin chimney. Two cars sat outside in a dirt driveway.

"Why don't we just call your CIA contacts and see if we can get an extraction team? Isn't that what they do?" Larsen asked.

"Not this far interior, they don't," Flynn said. "The battery on the sat phone is dying and we need to save any power we have for when we really need it. Let's just stay here for a few minutes and see what's going on."

All the lights in the cabin were still on, giving Flynn the impression that they were all awake. He preferred to hitch a ride with a kind-hearted man, but if they had to steal the car, so be it.

After a few minutes, the cabin door swung open and a young man strode onto the porch. He settled into a rocking chair and lit a cigarette. He took a long drag and stared out into the distance, almost looking right in their direction.

"How good is your Russian?" Flynn asked Knudsen.

"Serviceable."

"And your acting skills?"

She smiled. "I played Nora in A Doll's House in college, if that gives you any idea."

"The lead role? About a woman trying to find her way in a man's world?" Flynn said. "It's like you turned that character and story into your life."

"You wouldn't be that far from the truth," she said as she threw her cigarette down and extinguished it with her foot. "So, what role do you want me to play this time? Anything but the damsel in distress."

"I'm directing this drama, and right now, that's what I need," Flynn said with a sly grin. "Now march down that mountain and tell him that you and your two fellow comrades are desperate to get back to Finland tonight because of a family emergency, and Larsen here was going to drive you back but his car has a flat tire and it's too late to get it fixed properly."

She rolled her eyes. "You really think that's going to work?"

Flynn studied her closely before putting both hands on her blouse and ripping it open a few more inches.

"Flaunt it if you've got it," Flynn said.

"Is that a saying you have in America?" she asked.

He nodded. "It applies to many things in life, but it seemed like an appropriate time as ever to use that phrase."

She pushed her breasts up, revealing more cleavage.

"Is that enough for you?"

Flynn nodded. "No young man living out here will refuse you now."

She winked at him. "Or old man either," she said before heading toward the house.

"Old?" Flynn asked. "Did she just call me old?"

Larsen nodded. "There's no shame in being forty years old?"

"Me? You think I'm forty? Do I look that old to you?" Flynn said, his voice rising an octave with each question.

"Forty's the new black, right?" Larsen said.

Flynn sighed. "You do realize I'm actually a writer, correct? And there is no greater crime to the English language than mixing metaphors."

"Well, you know what they say about that, don't you?" Larsen said. "A bird in hand saves a stitch in time."

Flynn shoved Larsen playfully. "You better be glad she's down there trying to convince some young guy to give us a ride. Otherwise, I might just shoot you right here on the spot."

Larsen chuckled. "So, you're just giving me something to chew on?"

Flynn exhaled. "Finally, you got one right. I guess I'll let you live."

They both returned their attention to the house below where Knudsen was doing a great job of selling the young man on the idea of driving them. A few seconds later, she motioned for them to join her.

Flynn and Larsen hustled down the hill.

"Alexei and Ivan, I want you to meet my new friend, Mikhail," she said. "He's agreed to take us to a small village near the Finnish border for a small fee.

She grabbed the wallet from Larsen and fished out the money.

"I told him I thought five thousand rubles was a fair price."

"Sounds fair to me," Flynn said.

***

THREE HOURS LATER, Mikhail dropped off the trio forty-five kilometers east of Porosozero near the border in a rural farming region. Flynn believed they had traveled far enough away from the railway that they wouldn't have to be so guarded, especially at 3:00 a.m.

"Are we close enough to call an extraction team?" Larsen asked.

Flynn shook his head. "Not close enough yet. I'm sure Russian intelligence is trying to determine who did this. And once they finger us, we won't have much time."

"How far to the border?" Knudsen asked.

"By my calculations, I think we have about a thirty-kilometer hike."

Larsen shook his head. "We need to make it across before sunrise. And if these farmers are like the ones in Norway, it won't be long before they're awake."

"Do you think we can move at ten kilometers per hour over this terrain?" Flynn said.

Before anyone could answer, Flynn grabbed both of them by their shirts, yanking them backward.

"Do you hear that?" he said, putting his finger to his lips.

The silhouetted barn on a small hill approximately a hundred meters straight ahead was the source of the noise.

Flynn smiled. "Horses!"

They snuck up to the wooden structure and slipped inside. With a half dozen horses in their stables, Flynn knew they'd found a way to reach the border before daybreak.

"Help me saddle these up," Flynn said.

Larsen and Knudsen wasted no time in pulling gear off the wall and throwing it on top of the horses. In a matter of ten minutes, they'd managed to saddle up and were ready to ride.

Flynn had two more tasks to complete before they left. First, he needed to leave all of the cash in Berezin's wallet in a visible location to compensate the farmer, even though Flynn hoped the horses would be returned to the farm.

Next, he needed to secure the bag of seeds onto the saddle-bags. Once he finished, he mounted up.

"This adventure is almost over," Flynn said.

He pulled out his phone and found the coordinates on the GPS. Once he determined due west, they rode out the door and into the cool spring air.

They trotted along for an hour and a half in silence. Flynn wasn't sure if it was due to exhaustion or if they didn't really have anything else to say at that point. Or perhaps everyone simply enjoyed the sounds of nighttime nature.

An owl hooted in a tree overhead and a dog barked in the distance. Other than the constant sound of small creeks trickling along or the rustling of leaves, it felt almost eerie to Flynn. The serene sounds stood in stark contrast to the journey that had led them to that point.

He glanced at his watch and then at his GPS. The battery was running low, maybe thirty more minutes if he was lucky.

Then he froze.

"Do you hear that?" Flynn asked, pulling his horse to a stop.

Larsen and Knudsen followed suit and tried to remain still. The creaking of leather and a few scattered snorts from the horses was the only other sound to disturb the night.

"I don't hear anything," Larsen said.

"Me either," Knudsen added.

"I could've sworn I—"

Flynn stopped Larsen's sentence short, instead choosing to cover his eyes from the blinding light thrust upon him.

"Who are you?" said an elderly man in Russian. "What are you doing here?"

Larsen nodded to Flynn, signaling that he'd take the lead.

"I'm sorry, sir, but we're on an early morning ride. I hope we didn't disturb you," Larsen said.

"Those aren't your horses," the Russian man said.

He dropped the light so it wasn't shining directly at them.

In the moonlight, Flynn could make out a silhouette of the man along with a shotgun.

"I know who those horses belong to, and he won't be happy that you've taken them."

Flynn held up his hands.

"Please, sir, let me explain," Flynn said. "I'm sure you've heard of the impending food crisis, have you not?"

The man nodded. "All the corn in the U.S. is failing."

"Exactly, which is why we need to continue on our way across the border into Finland."

Before Flynn could continue, two more men wandered up the road, joining the farmer.

"I'm not sure I understand," the farmer said.

"The Russian military tried to steal the last remaining heirloom corn seeds belonging to—and native to—the U.S. However, we have it here."

"Am I supposed to care what you're doing?"

"If you care about avoiding a global food crisis, you should."

The farmer grunted and kicked at the dirt.

"Not my problem," he said.

One of the other men whispered in his ear.

"My friend tells me that he just heard on the radio about your escape."

The man whispered something else to the farmer.

"And there's a reward for any information leading to your capture, too."

"Sir, please, can you help us? You're a farmer. You care about crops and soil, don't you?"

The man shook his head. "I also care about a nice reward."

"People are going to die—thousands of them. We need to get these seeds back into the hands of people who can help farmers replant."

The farmer laughed. "You need to stay there until the military comes and picks you up so I can collect my reward. Do you understand?"

Flynn's satellite phone rang, creating a glow in his pants pocket.

"Careful," the farmer said. "I wouldn't want to have to shoot you."

Flynn held up his hands. "Let me turn off the ringer."

Jamming his hand inside his pocket, Flynn pushed a button on the phone, answering the call.

"So, where are we exactly?" Flynn said loudly. "About ten kilometers east of the Finland border near Möhkö?"

"It won't make any difference to you," the farmer said. "You'll be going to prison. I hear Siberia is a cruel place in the winter." He broke into a chuckle. "Even crueler than here."

"It's not that bad. Perhaps a few hundred meters from here would be a great spot to land."

The farmer shook his head. "I don't understand what you're talking about." He turned toward one of the men. "Go call the military and let them know we have the men they're pursuing—and their seeds."

CHAPTER 45

CIA Headquarters
Langley, VA

TODD OSBORNE PICKED UP on Flynn's clues. He put the call on speaker phone and furiously took notes, gathering as many overt and subtle clues as were dropped. If they were that close to the border, he might be able to scramble an extraction team in the air to rescue them. As Flynn continued talking, Osborne realized there were only three farmers holding them up. It certainly wasn't a handful of Russian operatives that would post a more difficult logistical problem as well as a political one.

He walked into the office of Gil Lawton, the deputy executive director.

"Want the good news or bad news first?" he asked

"Always the good news."

"Well, Flynn has the seeds and is only ten kilometers east of the Finland border."

"And the bad news?"

"They're being held at gunpoint by three Russian farmers."

Lawton smiled. "Now, that's the kind of bad news I like to hear."

"Think it's going to be that easy?"

"Easier than dealing with the Spetsnaz."

"You have a point. So, do you think we can scramble an extraction team to Flynn's position?"

Lawton shook his head. "I'm afraid he's on his own. We don't have any assets remotely close that could help."

CHAPTER 46

SENATOR POWELL CHECKED HIS WATCH and stared at the door. Phillip Wilson was already two minutes late. The clock on the wall ticked rhythmically, pushing Powell to the edge of insanity. Two weeks ago, Powell had made reservations to frequent his favorite restaurant, Charlie Palmer Steak, and enjoy a few glasses of wine on the balcony. Instead, he sat alone at home, wondering if Wilson would ever arrive.

Powell poured himself a drink and stared out the window, contemplating all that had gone wrong. Each decision he'd made since he took office weighed heavily on him. He never intended to reach this place where his legacy was defined by a series of decisions based on his desire to grab what he could. Yet he couldn't escape it now. Each vote, each trip, each conversation—they'd all become cemented in the annals of American politics. No matter what he did in the future, he couldn't erase what he'd already done.

But there was one thing he could do.

He picked up his gun and checked the chamber. It was loaded and ready to fire.

His relationship with Fenestra CEO Phillip Wilson was a complicated one, if not full of nuances and tight-rope walking. At least, that was how Powell saw it. He was desperate to make his mark on Washington, perhaps even run for president one day. But first he needed a way to grab the spotlight and make a name for himself. Wilson presented him with that opportunity.

The U.S. Senate Committee on Agriculture, Nutrition and Forestry wasn't exactly one Powell viewed as a pathway to exposure among the American people. Before he took over, it was widely viewed as a group of people who rubber stamped whatever was put before them. However, something changed a year into Powell's post as the committee chairman. Debates swirled over genetically modified crops as well as over the ethical implementation of patents on seeds. While Powell viewed his chair as a stepping stone to a more prominent committee, his had become the most talked about group on Capitol Hill for a few months while the national conversation about American crops and seeds reached a fever pitch.

Powell found himself on late night television shows as well as early morning news programs. The hosts varied in their political persuasion, but their questions seemed to remain centered on why Fenestra had been allowed to patent seeds and how it was affecting U.S. crops. They were interesting questions, many of which had been answered by lawyers and concerned parties many times over. But Powell had become a figurehead, the man associated with the simmering anger of farmers and consumers alike, none of whom wanted to be controlled by the whims of a company known for its Machiavellian approach to obtaining and enforcing patents.

That all felt like a hundred years ago to Powell, who ran his fingers along the contour of his handgun. He poured himself another drink and thought about how he should've declined Wilson's support years ago. But it was too late. Powell linked arms with Wilson and skipped off toward the pot of gold without a second thought. But Powell had given it a second, third, and fourth thought, and he concluded something needed to change.

Admitting to himself that it wasn't the ideal time to contemplate the ethical or moral dilemmas he faced, Powell forged ahead. He dashed down a path that wound around to a decidedly difficult conclusion: Powell held no strong convictions when it came to his votes or committee recommendations. No, he was just a puppet, masquerading as a thoughtful representative for the good people of California. His charade would've never started without people like Wilson in his life, trying to steer him down errant paths. It was time to sever that cord.

The doorbell startled Powell, snapping him out of his moment of regret and self loathing. He got up and sauntered to the front door, peeking through the curtains to see who the guest was. Phillip Wilson politely waved to him.

Powell shoved the gun into his pocket and opened the door.

"Come in, sir," Powell said. "Come in."

"Thank you," Wilson said as he took off his coat and hat. He handed them to Powell. "Will you see that they find a happy home here?"

"Certainly," Powell said, forcing a smile.

Powell hung up Wilson's clothes and ushered him into the sitting room.

"Would you like a drink?" Powell asked.

"Do you have any good scotch?"

"Nothing but the best."

"Good. Make mine a double then."

Powell poured a generous portion into the glass tumbler and handed it to Wilson.

"So, I assume this invitation wasn't just a social call."

Powell shook his head.

Wilson took a long pull on his drink.

"Don't keep me in suspense any longer. Out with it."

"Have a seat," Powell said, gesturing to the couch across from him. Both men sat down cautiously, careful not to spill their drinks.

"You have quite a knack for building up the anticipation," Wilson said with a laugh.

Powell set his drink down on the end table next to his chair and leaned forward in his seat.

"First, I want to begin by thanking you, Phillip. You've been so instrumental in helping me navigate my early days in Washington and I'm eternally grateful."

Wilson smiled. "Just doing my job."

Powell abruptly stood up and paced for a few steps before stopping and pointing at Wilson.

"That's exactly what I was afraid of."

"What?"

"You doing your job when it came to me."

Wilson furrowed his brow. "I'm not sure I understand."

Powell resumed pacing. "You're no fool, that much I've come to realize. When I arrived in Washington, I have no doubt that you foresaw the shit storm brewing for Fenestra. In this great age of information—and misinformation—you knew that people were going to be railing against your company. There were going to be concerns, some legitimate and some not, about how you conducted your business. The playing God with the genetics of seeds and the enforcement of patent laws when it came to farmers. You sent me out to the front lines before the battle even began as a peacekeeper. You wanted me to quell the dissent bubbling beneath the surface long enough for Fenestra to develop a lobby so powerful that it couldn't be stopped."

"Now, Dan, I think you're reading into things too much."

Powell stopped and pointed at Wilson again.

"Let me finish. I have a few more things to say."

Wilson threw his hands in the air and leaned back on the couch.

"Go on. Say your peace."

"This isn't about saying my piece," Powell continued. "This is about me helping you realize I know what you were doing. To be honest, I didn't at the time, but I finally figured it all out. The trips, the introductions, the gifts. You leveraged everything you could to coerce me into becoming your loyal lapdog."

Powell broke into a slow clap and continued.

"Well, congratulations, Phillip, because it worked."

"I'm afraid that's not how it went down at all. I mean, yes, I was looking for an ally on the Hill to help with our cause, but I picked you because I saw a man who had the guts to do the right thing for the common good, even when it wasn't easy."

"Is that what you tell yourself so you can sleep at night?"

"If it weren't for all the technological advances we've made in seed development and creating crops resistant to pests, we might not be able to feed the world like we have been—or at best, everything would cost more. I never manipulated you for the purposes of advancing Fenestra's cause. You did that all on your own."

Powell balled up his fist, shaking with anger as he put it close to his mouth.

"How could I have done that on my own? I didn't even know what I was doing. Admit it: You gave me gentle nudges along with a few hard shoves to get me going in the direction you needed me to go. You didn't get to be the CEO of a company valued at 800 million dollars without some shrewd business tactics."

"I can tell you're upset—and I must confess that it's been a rough few days for everyone in the city, hell, in this country. But I've got a way out of this."

"Do you now? I'm starting to wonder if this whole thing wasn't orchestrated by you to try and drive up corn prices."

Wilson sighed. "Oh, come on. I'd never do something like that. Have you seen the PR hit we've taken over the past week or so? What vested CEO would do that to his company?"

"Only a CEO longing to go to prison would defy an agreement with a senate committee, which is illegal in case you didn't know."

"We only injected the terminator gene into those crops because we knew we couldn't trust those farmers who were stealing from us. If they hadn't tried to get away with something, no one would've ever known—and it wouldn't have mattered anyway."

"Always justifying your actions instead of taking responsibility for them. Who do you think you are? A congressman?"

"Just try and see it from my perspective. I only did what any sane CEO would do: Anything I could to save my company."

Sitting down across from Wilson, Powell took hold of the gun in his pocket.

"That's just it," Powell said. "You're not sane. You're crazy. And it wouldn't shock me to learn that you were behind everything that just happened, though I haven't been able to figure out how or why."

He pulled the gun out and set it on the coffee table between them.

Wilson's eyes widened as he stared at the weapon.

"What's that for?" he said, withdrawing into the couch.

"It's going to help me put an end to all your puppetry once and for all."

"Wha—" Wilson said.

Powell proceeded to lunge for the gun, beating Wilson to it. Powell inspected it, holding it up to the light for a few moments.

"I'm done with you," Powell said as he glanced at Wilson. "You've spent far too long dictating how I'm going to live my life."

With the gun trained on Wilson, Powell steadied it with two hands.

Wilson shook as he threw his hands in the air.

"Come on, Dan, you don't want to do this, do you? I've got a way out of this."

"It's illegal, I'm sure."

"We'd take a PR hit, I'm sure, but not illegal. I can solve this."

Powell huffed in disgust. "I'm sure you can solve it in

your own deviant way. But I'm done with it. I don't need you to solve anything else for me."

Wilson put his hands out, his voice quivering. "If you kill me, your life, such as it is, will be over."

Powell eyed him closely.

"Who said anything about killing you?"

Without hesitating, Powell jammed the barrel of his gun into his own forehead.

"At least you'll get to see what freedom looks like," Powell said. "This is going to be me showing you—"

"You're phone is ringing," Wilson said, his voice still quaking. "Please answer it. I—I know there's nothing I can say that will make you change your mind, but maybe the person on the other end of that call is someone who cares about you. Maybe—maybe it's someone you want to say goodbye to."

"Those people have been out of my life for quite some time now."

Powell clicked off the safety on his gun.

Wilson grabbed the phone and answered it, putting it on speakerphone.

"Hello?" Wilson said.

"Powell? Is that you?" came a familiar voice. It was CIA agent Todd Osborne.

"Yeah, it's me," Powell said, wearing a look of disgust and disappointment on his face. "What do you want?"

"You told me to call you when I heard from our operative."

"And?"

"I need your help to save him."

Powell's face broke into a faint smile.

CHAPTER 47

Northwest, Russia

FYNN EYED THE TWO FARMERS armed with shotguns standing about ten meters across from them in the rickety barn. With all the unforgiving winters in that portion of Russia, Flynn was surprised anyone chose to live there. He shifted his weight from side to side while staring at the stable floor scattered with hay and horse manure. Flynn grabbed the door and rattled it, testing the strength of the padlock. It held fast.

The farmers both shook their heads as they leaned against two stacks of resources necessary to survive: chopped wood and bales of hay. They were both stacked floor to ceiling, already in preparation for the coming winter. Flynn figured it took a special kind of person to gut out the bitter cold year after year, the kind of person who specialized in stubbornness. But Flynn had to try something to persuade the farmers to let him and his friends go on their way.

"Do you have any children?" Flynn asked, standing on his toes to see over the top of the stable gate.

One of the farmers shook his head while the other nodded.

"I've got six children, all good workers on this farm," one farmer said.

"Surely you wouldn't want them to starve, would you?" Flynn responded.

"Nobody on this farm is going to starve. We have enough food stored up to last two years or more."

"But what if someone raided your storehouse? Then what?"

The farmer shook his head, refusing to play along with Flynn.

"What now?" Larsen whispered. "We don't even know where the seeds are."

Knudsen, who'd been crouching in the corner, crawled over to them.

"I know where they are," she whispered. "I watched through the slats and saw one of the men put the seeds in that shed near his house. He put our guns there, too."

"That still leaves us nowhere when it comes to getting out of here," Larsen said. "Got any ideas?"

Flynn nodded. "Kari, how strong is that barn wall?"

"What do you mean?" she said.

"Could we bust through it?"

She shrugged. "It's possible. If anything, we might be able to rip it apart."

He pointed toward the wall. "Go check."

She eased over to the wall and pressed against it. She stopped when she felt it start to give way. Once she returned to Flynn and Larsen, she reported her findings.

"I think we can get through it."

"Think or know?" Flynn asked again.

"Know."

"Good because my plan hinges on it."

He shared the details of the plan and told everyone to get ready.

"What if this doesn't work?" Larsen asked.

"If you've got a better idea, let's have it," Flynn snapped.

Larsen shook his head. "But just for the record, I'm not very fond of this plan."

"Your lack of fondness has been noted. Now get ready."

Flynn and Larsen gathered as much hay as they could find and piled it together. Knudsen knelt at the back of the stable and looked outside to see if there was any movement in the barnyard.

When Flynn and Larsen finished building their stack, Flynn got Larsen's attention.

"Psst. Anything?"

She flashed him a thumbs up.

"You ready?" Flynn asked Larsen.

"Again, I'd like to express—"

"Save it for later and get ready to run."

Flynn took the lighter Knudsen had lifted from the train car, flicking it alive. He carefully held it near the bottom of the pile and blew gently onto the burgeoning strands, which began to smolder. He repeated this process at several different locations around the pile until it was roaring.

"Time to invoke those acting skills again," Flynn said to Knudsen.

She stood up and started screaming.

"Fire! Fire! Help!"

The two farmers rushed toward them, but the blaze had already jumped from the hay to the stable door.

"Help!" Knudsen called again.

"Now!" Flynn said.

All three of them tore across the stable, putting their

shoulders into the wall at the same time. Their momentum carried them through the wall as they tumbled on the ground outside the barn. They trio wasted no time in leaping to their feet and racing toward the shed. Flynn and Larsen planned to get the seeds, while Knudsen was in charge of the weapons.

A shotgun fired, ripping through the air as the fire crackled in the barn behind them.

Flynn glanced over his shoulder and saw the farmer who'd just shot in their direction rush back toward the barn.

A few moments later, the other farmer who'd gone into his house to contact the authorities rushed back outside and started yelling at them. Two more gunshots rang out.

Less than five seconds later, they were rummaging through the shed looking for their guns—and the seeds.

"Where is it?" Larsen said. "I thought you said it was in here."

Knudsen dug through tools stacked in a bin. "I saw him put them inside here."

"Are you sure?" Larsen asked.

"Yes. I know what I saw."

"Well, it's not in here."

Flynn then let out a victorious yelp. "Found 'em."

He dished out the wares and glanced back through the doorway, where he could see one farmer storming toward them with a gun pointed in their direction.

"Allow me," Knudsen said, nudging Flynn to the side.

She steadied her gun against the doorjamb and squeezed off a shot.

The farmer stumbled to the ground, wallowing in pain.

"Just a flesh wound," she said to Flynn, who was scowling at her. "He doesn't deserve the same fate as Commander Berezin."

They wasted no more time, sprinting out of the shed toward a flatbed truck about ten meters away.

Cramming inside the small cab, Flynn was pleasantly surprised to find the keys in the ignition.

He turned the key as the truck roared to life. Instinctively, he returned to the road and headed farther east toward what he believed to be the border. They bumped along the road for twenty minutes as the sun started to cast its first rays of light on the surrounding area they'd only experienced in the dark for the past seven hours.

Larsen rolled down his window.

"What is it?" Flynn said.

Then he rolled his down too and heard it.

"Choppers."

"How far do you think we are from the border?" Larsen asked.

"Not far," he said. "I'm just hoping this road will take us close enough to it."

The helicopter beats grew louder until Flynn realized they were right behind them. Flynn jammed his foot on the pedal and gripped the steering wheel hard.

A smile trickled across his face as he read the Russian road sign ahead.

It was faded like most things in that part of the country, but it warned drivers to prepare to show their passport. Despite another sign warning him to slow down, Flynn kept the gas pedal depressed. He looked out of the window up at the helicopter, which had descended and was hovering about ten meters above them.

"Are you going to slow down?" Knudsen asked.

"At this point, I don't think that's an opt—"

Flynn halted his thoughts as he slammed on the brakes. The truck skidded for a few meters, screeching until it came to a stop.

He stared at the dilapidated bridge in front of them that was out. Finland was so close he could literally see it, though it was obvious that the border crossing had long since been abandoned. A barrier in front of the short bridge, along with barbed wire coils atop a fence stretching along the Russian side of the ravine, made it clear.

The helicopter descended all the way down to the road, hovering less than a meter off the ground. A man spoke over a loudspeaker, instructing them to get out of the vehicle.

Flynn sighed and scanned the area for an exit strategy.

"Great. What do we do now?" Larsen said.

Flynn shook his head. "We're trapped."

CHAPTER 48

Omsk, Russia

GROMOV GREW IMPATIENT with his lack of contact from Commander Berezin. Gromov should've heard from him hours ago, but instead Gromov was finishing a bottle of wine. Against his better judgment, he stumbled downstairs into the wine cellar to look for more.

"What are you doing, dear?" Irina asked, calling from upstairs.

"I'm fine," he said.

He spent ten minutes mulling over his choices before concluding he didn't prefer any of the vintage years. He made a mental note to restock his cellar with wine from 1964, specifically his favorite, the Petrus Pomerol. However, he wasn't certain he'd actually remember after the alcohol wore off.

Once he returned upstairs, he slumped into his chair. He checked his phone and no one had called.

"Stop looking so depressed," Irina said as she entered the room. "What could possibly make a man in your position and wealth so upset?"

"You wouldn't understand."

"I wouldn't? Or you don't want to tell me?"

He stood up and stomped off to his study, slamming the door behind him.

Pacing around the room, he considered what to do next. He opened his laptop and read a news story about a trio of escaped prisoners from a Russian base. The report didn't identify their nationalities, but it made Gromov nervous as he started to piece together what he knew and feared the worse.

Berezin had been explicitly clear that Gromov was not to call him under any circumstances. It was how he wanted to conceal what they were doing. Berezin was going to report that he destroyed the seeds, but he needed to ensure that no one could place him in contact with Gromov. Berezin would make a quick exchange at the train depot with one of his trusted soldiers, who would then drop the seeds at a location he and Gromov had previously decided. The soldier making the drop wouldn't even know the contents of the package.

But Berezin was supposed to have checked in hours ago—and he hadn't.

Gromov decided that if Berezin was breaking protocol, so would he. Dialing Berezin's number, Gromov continued to pace around the room as he waited for someone to answer.

"Privyet?" came the unfamiliar voice from a man.

"Commander Berezin?"

"Nyet."

Gromov hesitated, unsure if he should hang up or ask another question. His curiosity prevented him from doing what he knew he should've done.

"Where is Commander Berezin?"

"He's dead. Who is this?"

Gromov hung up and threw the phone at his reading chair on the other side of the room. His plan had gone sideways and there was no way to hide his intentions.

He could only hope there wouldn't be repercussions.

CHAPTER 49

Russia-Finland Border

FLYNN WHEELED THE TRUCK around so that it faced the helicopter. Another announcement from the pilot came across strong and forceful. They had one minute to surrender or they would open fire. The Russian Mi-24 hovered low to the ground and awaited the trio's next move.

"What now?" Larsen asked. "I'm not interested in getting gunned to death this close to the border."

"So you'd rather go to a Russian prison? Let me tell you something: you'd rather do anything else," Knudsen said.

Flynn remained focused on figuring out a solution.

"What's in the back of the truck? Anything useful?" he asked.

"Nothing we can weaponize, if that's what you mean," Larsen answered.

"What about a brick?"

"There's a cinder block," Knudsen said.

"Can you reach through the window and grab it for me?"

Larsen nodded. "I think so."

Flynn started to tear the bottom of his shirt.

"What are you doing?" Knudsen asked.

"Still have that lighter?" Flynn asked her.

She nodded and handed it to him.

"Good," Flynn said. "It's our ticket out of here."

Larsen pulled the cinder block through and set it at his feet.

"What do you want me to do with this?" he asked.

"Hand it to me."

Larsen passed it over to Flynn, who shoved the truck into park and proceeded to rev up the engine.

"When I give the signal, we're going to open our doors and back away from the truck slowly. Both of you grab a bag of seeds out of the back while I'm going to turn this truck into a bomb."

"What are you going to do?" Knudsen asked.

"Don't worry about me. Do you understand what I've asked you to do?"

They both nodded.

"Good."

Flynn revved up the engine again.

"Go!"

Larsen and Knudsen exited slowly from the passenger side, using the door as a shield. They crept backward and stayed low to the ground. Larsen reached into the truck bed and yanked a bag of seeds out before handing it to Knudsen. He pulled the other bag out as they both moved behind the back of the truck.

Meanwhile, Flynn had eased out of the driver's side and snuck back to the gas tank. He shoved the portion of his shirt he'd cut into the gas tank and let it soak for a few seconds before retrieving it.

"You got the bags?" Flynn asked.

"Yes," Larsen answered.

"Good. Get ready to run."

Flynn shoved the rag back into the gas tank with about half a meter sticking outside. He lit the end of the rag and rushed to the driver's side where the door was still open. Dropping the cinder block on the accelerator, he glanced back at the rag where the fire had raced about halfway up it headed for the tank. He then put the truck into drive and joined Larsen and Knudsen.

The truck sped away, directly toward the helicopter. The Mi-24 opened fire on the truck, unleashing a pair of missiles at it.

"Run!" Flynn yelled.

He didn't look back once he caught up with Larsen and Knudsen, who were both racing away from the truck.

Flynn didn't see the fiery explosion where the truck soared ten meters into the air before coming down the ground with a thud. A few seconds later, another missile from the helicopter rocked the ground. But Flynn was only focused on escaping across the border.

The trio slid down the ravine toward the Anninkoski River. Its peaceful flow stood in stark contrast to the earth-shaking explosions occurring less than a hundred meters away.

Flynn heard another low humming noise. He looked up to see a Bell 412 helicopter hovering on the Finnish side of the border.

A cord dropped from the helicopter, and a man harnessed to the rope descended to the bank of the river.

"Ready to go home?" the man asked. "Lieutenant General Pedersen is ready to get you there."

Flynn nodded. He sent Knudsen and Larsen up first along with the bags of seeds. When it was his turn, Flynn ascended and stared at the Russian helicopter. It had destroyed the truck and avoided getting damaged by the explosion, but it could only watch as the precious cargo escaped. For all Russia's posturing to reassert its dominance in the international community, it still couldn't afford to start a war.

Flynn gave a mock salute, first with his hand and then with his middle finger.

CHAPTER 50

Oslo, Norway

FLYNN DIDN'T THINK it was possible for him to be so emotional when it came time to say goodbye to Knudsen and Larsen. Their mission had become their single focus, yet in the process of fulfilling it, they'd become bonded for life.

"I hope you don't get lung cancer, but I sure am glad you smoke," Flynn said as he hugged Knudsen.

She smiled, tucking her hair behind her ears.

"I told you that I only smoke when I get stressed out."

"Well, I hope you never have to smoke again."

She laughed softly. "That's not likely. Life on Svalbard is always an adventure."

Flynn gave Larsen a hearty hug next.

"You're going to get an epic review on Travel Advisor, I can promise you that."

Larsen smiled. "Make it sound real."

"I don't know how I can. But I appreciate you sticking with me. I know I couldn't have done this without you. I'd probably be dead somewhere back there in a Russian field, if I'd even made it that far."

"You wouldn't have made it that far," Larsen quipped.

Flynn grabbed Larsen's bicep and squeezed it.

"Thanks."

"It was my pleasure," Larsen said. "You know I'm always looking for great stories to tell to my next set of clients in the Arctic."

"They won't believe you."

Larsen chuckled. "They never do."

Flynn followed one of the crew members up the steps of the C-130. Buckling his seat belt, Flynn glanced at the two bags of seeds secured to the plane floor just a few meters away. He struggled to believe that those two bags meant so much, not only to his country but also the world.

"Can I borrow your phone?" Flynn asked the airman seated next to him.

The man dug it out of his pocket and handed it to Flynn.

Flynn went straight to his favorite news site to get a bead on what was happening back home. On the front page of the site, an article trumpeted how the impending doom projected by so many people had been mitigated due to a covert U.S. operation to reclaim the seeds from a group that sought to steal them. Flynn thought it was interesting that the reporter didn't name Russia as the country that had stolen the seeds. Or maybe they didn't know. Either way, it didn't truly matter. The situation was as good as ancient history.

The next article he read explained how U.S. officials were projecting that corn production would suffer significantly in the coming months but be restored to eighty percent within the next twelve months. Senior analysts in Wall Street predicted that it would be good enough to ease prices and the projected shortage in various industries.

Flynn asked the airman if he could make a call. The airman gave him the okay.

"Theresa, it's me, Flynn."

Theresa Thompson, Flynn's editor at The National, exhaled.

"I was hoping to hear from you soon since I learned that you were the one chasing down the seeds across the Arctic."

"Who told you about that?"

"It's not important. But I am curious if you've got a story for me."

"Oh, I've got a story, but it's not exactly one you can print."

"You're worthless, Flynn."

Flynn sighed. "So I help save the world but don't have a story and I'm worthless."

"To me you are. Hurry home so I can give you an assignment that won't have so much danger involved."

"You're the one who made my last assignment, not me."

"We'll talk when you get back."

Flynn hung up and watched the turbo prop engines fire up. The blades cut through the still air with precision and speed. He watched as one of the crew members on the ground pulled the blocks away from the wheel.

The plane lurched forward and started to slowly roll down the runway.

"One more thing," Flynn said, holding up the phone to the airman.

"Whatever you need," he said. "This isn't a commercial flight."

Flynn navigated back to his favorite news site and looked up the financial section and scanned for articles about futures commodities.

"Wheat Down 80 Percent," blared one headline.

"Russian Farmers Panicking," heralded another.

Flynn clicked the phone off and handed it back to his fellow passenger.

The plane's nose jerked upward, and Flynn was thrust back against his seat. He watched out the window as Oslo disappeared beneath them while the plane climbed higher. In a matter of minutes, Norway's majestic fjords and mountain peaks vanished.

Flynn could barely see the ground for all the puffy white clouds extending seemingly forever toward the horizon. He enjoyed the view, admiring its beauty and apparently infinite pattern. It was the first time he'd relaxed in almost a week. And he deserved it.

CHAPTER 51

Omsk, Russia

GROMOV REMAINED SILENT when Irina asked the question for a second time. She simply wanted to know what island he was considering to purchase. Her demand wasn't outrageous or antagonistic, just a question.

If she only knew …

Gromov had a hunch about what might happen next, though he was reluctant to believe his own prophetic inclinations. He read the articles on international websites and heard the reports on Russian news. But he didn't want to believe them. He didn't want to believe that Berezin had failed to deliver the seeds, much less that they were back in the hands of the Americans. He couldn't accept it—or at least, didn't want to.

"What is wrong with you today?" Irina said. "Didn't you hear my question?"

He waved her off dismissively.

"Don't treat me like that."

Gromov grabbed her arms and shook her briefly.

"Treat you like what? I obviously don't want to answer your question. Maybe it's a surprise."

She rolled her eyes. "If it were a surprise, you would at least treat me with some common decency. It's called respect."

He grunted and turned his back on her.

"And apparently, you will not give me any."

He wandered into his study and turned on his computer. Plopping down into his chair, he read a news story about how Russian farmers were plowing their summer wheat under, concluding that it wasn't even worth it. A related story appeared on the same page about how Gromov Global would likely be unable to survive the current crisis. With wheat prices the lowest they'd be in almost fifty years without inflation, the article projected Russian farmers would turn to new cash crops in order to survive in the coming years.

Gromov let out a string of expletives before he slammed his laptop down.

"What do they know?"

If Gromov was honest with himself, he was more concerned with how the Russian government might respond to his collusion with Commander Berezin to re-sell the seeds to an American corporation. But he didn't want to think about it. He'd deal with it when that day came.

He poured himself a drink from his latest shipment of wine, a 1964 Petrus Pomerol. Savoring every flavor, he swirled it around in his mouth before swallowing it.

There's never been a more perfect wine.

Gromov walked out onto the veranda, still swirling the wine around in his glass. His plans hadn't panned out the way he'd hoped, but it wasn't time to plunge into deep despair. He'd figure a way out of it.

He took another long pull on his wine glass before he waved at a pair of kayakers on the river below. But instead of receiving the customary return wave, the lead kayaker put his oars down and pulled out another object—a gun.

In two quick seconds, the kayaker peppered Gromov's veranda with a dozen rounds, three of which hit Gromov.

Gromov staggered to the ground, dropping his glass of wine. He looked up at Irina, who had a panicked look on her face, one that was quickly replaced by a painful look when another bullet plowed into her chest.

She collapsed in a heap on top of him, both left to bleed out, compliments of the Spetsnaz.

CHAPTER 52

WHEN FLYNN'S PLANE TOUCHED DOWN at Andrews Air Force Base, he felt safe for the first time in over a week. Traversing the Arctic and the northwest corner of Russia was far more excitement than he'd bargained for when his editor assigned him to a simple story about The Global Seed Vault in Svalbard. Without anything other than a paperback book he'd picked up while in Norway waiting to be flown back to the U.S., Flynn walked at a measured pace as he descended the ladder leading to the tarmac.

A military communications officer hustled over to him and held out a phone.

"The president would like to speak with you, Mr. Flynn," the officer said.

Flynn took the phone.

"This is James Flynn."

"Mr. Flynn, I wanted to be the first to call you and give you a hearty congratulations for serving your country so admirably."

"I hope it's what anyone in my situation would've done."

The president laughed softly. "If they could have,

296 | R.J. PATTERSON

maybe. But you went above and beyond, putting others first. And that is to be commended."

"Thank you, sir. I do care about others."

"Well, I'd love to share your acts of courage with the rest of the nation in a ceremony at the Rose Garden later this week."

"I appreciate the gesture, Mr. President, but I'd like to politely decline. My life is far too public for my liking as it is, and making me into some kind of hero is only going to exacerbate that problem."

"Very well then. I'm not going to ignore the polite request of an American hero."

"You're far too kind, Mr. President."

"No, I'm not. In fact, if you ever want to write about the White House, you just let me know. I'll be as accommodating as possible."

"Now, that's something I just might take you up on, sir."

"Since you won't let the rest of America salute you, I'm saluting you for the rest of the country. Well done, Mr. Flynn."

"Thank you again, Mr. President."

The line went dead, and Flynn handed the phone back to the communications officer.

***

ON MONDAY, Flynn ventured into The National's Washington, D.C. bureau to meet with his editor, Theresa Thompson.

She was tapping her pen on her desk and poring over some papers when Flynn knocked on her door.

"Come in," she said, without even looking up.

"I didn't expect a hero's welcome, but I figured you'd at

least look up at me," Flynn said.

She stopped and stood up. She walked around her desk to give Flynn a hug.

"I'm glad you made it back alive," she said. "I was starting to get worried when I hadn't heard from you. We even posted a story about you on our online portal."

"I hope someone told you."

She smiled and nodded her head. "Your pal from the CIA notified me about what was going on and suggested some language for us to use on our website to let all our readers know that you were safe and no harm had come to you."

"When was this?"

"About five days ago."

Flynn shook his head. "Five days ago? Really? That was right when I was being held in a prison located in the bowels of a Russian military base."

"Agent Osborne must have a great deal of faith in you."

"He shouldn't. I got out of there by the skin of my teeth."

"But you got out of there—and you saved the country in the process, maybe even the world."

"Don't make this thing bigger than it already is."

She chuckled. "Have a seat. We need to talk about how to proceed."

Flynn sat down. "Proceed? What are you suggesting? That I write about this adventure?"

"Of course. It'll sell millions of copies and get millions more eyeballs on our website."

"Are you aware that when I reached Svalbard, I met a guy in the baggage claim section of the airport wearing a sweatshirt with the Illuminati eye? He asked me who I was and told me that I looked familiar—then he freaked out. It's bad enough that I'm a hero to conspiracy nuts. Now you want to make me some action hero that everyone will know and recognize? No thank you."

"Do you think you can get me one of those sweat-shirts?" Thompson said, tongue-in-cheek.

"I swear—"

"Okay, calm down. I won't reveal your name, but could you at least let us tell the story?"

"Let me talk with the CIA first and then ask them what details they feel comfortable releasing. The Russians have probably already figured out who I am, if they didn't know at the time, but I still prefer my anonymity."

"Fair enough, but I want the exclusive info first from the CIA."

"I think I can arrange that."

"Good, but I still need that story on The Global Seed Vault."

"You are aware that I didn't get hardly any information."

"I know. That's why I'm sending you back next week."

Flynn stood up. "Anything else?"

"Yeah," she said, staring out the window. "I lead a boring life, don't I?"

A wry grin spread across Flynn's face.

"Not everyone can save the world like me."

He winked at her and exited the office.

***

FLYNN FLOPPED DOWN ON HIS COUCH and binged on the news, trying to catch up with the story that was still spinning. Despite the fact that he'd rescued the heirloom seeds, there was still going to be a severe corn shortage in the coming year. It'd likely be mitigated for the next season, but in the meantime, farmers, manufacturers, and consumers alike would all have to deal with the fallout.

The talking heads at the news desk tried to allay fears that the world would dive into a worldwide food crisis.

"Thankfully, the United States has the best special ops program on the planet, and they were able to retrieve the last known samples of heirloom corn seeds in the U.S.," the TV personality said.

If they only knew it was a bunch of Norwegians who saved my ass so many times.

The next related story detailed how the FBI had captured Noah Barton, the man responsible for arson that destroyed all of Fenestra's corn-growing facilities. However, due to the urgency of the situation, multiple contractors banded together and projected to have the facilities fully restored to working order within two weeks.

The anchor then added an interesting note that federal investigators discovered that Barton's operation was being funded by wealthy Russian businessman Yury Gromov, who was also found dead along with his wife in what Russian authorities were calling a botched robbery attempt.

Botched robbery attempt? I wonder what Gromov was up to.

The final story of the segment was about one of California's U.S. Senators, Dan Powell. For his tight relationship with Fenestra, Powell was widely rebuked for his actions, some even blaming him for the impending corn crisis. His legislation record was more than favorable to Fenestra, and people took note. However, a report from the president's office detailed that Powell was the one largely responsible for ensuring that the U.S.'s seeds were rightfully returned to American soil. Given the timing of the report, it was also odd that Powell had just announced that he would not seek re-election. The reporter explained that there was a rumor that Powell was in the running to replace the Secretary of State, who'd recently declared his intention to step down. The segment ended with the president's announcement of a new oversight committee for the FDA, which would help develop a more advanced approach to sussing out non-traditional terrorist attacks that "threatened the American way of life."

Sounds like another big conspiracy waiting to happen.

Flynn turned the television off, not even bothering to get dressed for bed. It was all catching up with him—every last second he'd abdicated sleep on purpose or against his will.

Less than five minutes later, he was snoring and wouldn't wake up until well after noon the next day.

CHAPTER 53

Monday, May 14
Longyearbyen, Svalbard

FLYNN OPENED THE DOOR at The Arctic Barrel and strode inside. The pub seemed exactly as it had a couple of weeks ago when he first sat down and tried to get a meal there. Everyone was enjoying the never-ending daylight hours, and he couldn't wait to join them.

He slid into a bench next to Larsen, who shook with surprise.

"Bloody hell, if it isn't James Flynn," Larsen said as he put his arm around Flynn. "What are you doing here?"

Flynn winked at Knudsen, who was sitting across from Larsen with a pint in her hand.

"I still have a story to write," Flynn began, "and I was wondering if either of you could help get me up to speed on the story of The Global Seed Vault and its impact on the community here on Svalbard."

Knudsen smiled. "I think it's far more important than we know, not just to Svalbard but also to the rest of the world."

Flynn grabbed an untouched glass of water and held it up, inviting Larson and Knudsen to clink their glasses to his.

Before another word could be uttered, a young man in his twenties rushed into the pub and ran up to their table.

"Sysselmannen Knudsen, there's been an accident on Hopen Island that requires immediate medical help and treatment," he said, gasping for breath.

"A polar bear incident?" she asked.

He nodded.

She looked at Flynn and Larsen.

"So, who's up for another adventure?"

THE END

Acknowledgments

GETTING TO WRITE a story that practically started in my backyard proved to be more fun—and challenging—than I thought possible. However, I still needed to lean on the assistance and expertise of plenty of people in cobbling together this tale.

For starters, without readers who have found my work—and enjoyed it—I never would have trudged on with the arduous task of writing novels. Just knowing that you're out there, enjoying the diversions created by my books, inspires me to press on and work diligently to refine my craft.

The good people at The Experimental Breeder Reactor I in eastern Idaho helped me gain a better understanding of the terrain and environment from which this story launched.

David Doeringsfeld, the port manager at the Port of Lewiston, was patient in explain the inner workings of port life along the river at Idaho's only seaport.

Kelly Stimpert and some of her colleagues at the CDC equipped me on how to write intelligently (I hope) about the creation of vaccines and antidotes.

As with almost all my writing projects, Jennifer Wolf's editing helped make this a better story. Without her, this novel might be more confusing, not to mention full of female characters wearing horribly matched clothes.

Dan Pitts crafted and conceived another brilliant cover.

Bill Cooper continues to produce stellar audio versions of all my books — and have no doubt that this will yield the same high-quality listening enjoyment.

And last, but certainly not least, I must acknowledge my wife and her gracious soul for allowing me to once again immerse myself in a world of my own making while I wrote this story, one I hope you truly enjoyed.

About the Author

R.J. PATTERSON is a national award-winning journalist and award-winning author living in the Pacific Northwest. He first began his illustrious writing career as a sports journalist, recording his exploits on the soccer fields in England as a young boy. Then when his father told him that people would pay him to watch sports if he would write about what he saw, he went all in. He landed his first writing job at age 15 as a sports writer for a daily newspaper in Orangeburg, S.C. He later earned a degree in newspaper journalism from the University of Georgia, where he took a job covering high school sports for the award-winning *Athens Banner-Herald* and *Daily News*.

He later became the sports editor of *The Valdosta Daily Times* before working in the magazine world as an editor and freelance journalist. He has won numerous writing awards, including a national award for his investigative reporting on a sordid tale surrounding an NCAA investigation over the University of Georgia football program.

R.J. enjoys the great outdoors of the Northwest while living there with his wife and three children. He still follows sports closely.

He also loves connecting with readers and would love to hear from you. To stay updated about future projects, connect with him over Facebook or on the Internet at www.RJPbooks.com.

Others Books in the James Flynn Series

The Warren Omissions
Imminent Threat
The Cooper Affair
Seeds of War